W9-BBC-579

discord

Schmaling Mem. Pub. Library
501 Tenth Avenue
Fulton, IL 61252

SHOWDOWN AT ANCHOR

Center Point
Large Print

Also by Peter Dawson and available from
Center Point Large Print:

Troublesome Range
Posse Guns
Willow Basin

**This Large Print Book carries the
Seal of Approval of N.A.V.H.**

SHOWDOWN AT ANCHOR

A WESTERN QUINTET

PETER DAWSON

CENTER POINT LARGE PRINT
THORNDIKE, MAINE

This Center Point Large Print edition is published
in the year 2015 by arrangement with
Golden West Literary Agency.

Copyright © 2005 by Dorothy S. Ewing.

Additional copyright information on page 291.

All rights reserved.

The text of this Large Print edition is unabridged.
In other aspects, this book may vary
from the original edition.
Printed in the United States of America
on permanent paper.
Set in 16-point Times New Roman type.

ISBN: 978-1-62899-564-0 (hardcover)
ISBN: 978-1-62899-569-5 (paperback)

Library of Congress Cataloging-in-Publication Data

Dawson, Peter, 1907–1957.
[Short stories. Selections]
Showdown at anchor : a western quintet / Peter Dawson. —
    Center Point Large Print edition.
pages cm
Summary: "The heart of the American West lives in five stories with
characters that blaze a trail over a land of frontier dreams and
nightmares and across a country coming of age and filled with
conflicts"—Provided by publisher.
 ISBN 978-1-62899-564-0 (hardcover : alk. paper)
 ISBN 978-1-62899-569-5 (pbk. : alk. paper)
 1. Large type books.
    I. Dawson, Peter, 1907–1957. Tinhorn takes a tank town. II. Title.
PS3507.A848A6 2015b
813′.52—dc23
                                                    2015003686

SHOWDOWN AT ANCHOR

TABLE OF CONTENTS

A Tinhorn Takes a Tank Town

This story under this title was submitted by Jon Glidden's agent to Street & Smith's *Western Story Magazine* on July 17, 1937. Certain editorial changes were requested, and these were duly made by the author. The revised version was submitted on December 22, 1937. In its revised form, the story was accepted for publication January 10, 1938 and the story appeared in the issue dated April 9, 1938. The author was paid $135 upon publication.

I

It had taken him eight days to make the ride to Gunflash, and here, where the town's single street swung to face the foot of the ridge, High-Card Stevens reined in at the tie rail in front of the sheriff's office. Eight days ago he had sold out his table at Riley's in Tombstone. He had shed his frock coat and now wore a cowpuncher's waist overalls and denim shirt. His lean face had taken on a deeper bronze than usual, so that by contrast his eyes seemed to have lightened in shade from slate to the color of clear ice. He wore one gun, not in a shoulder holster as was his habit when gambling, but in the more familiar position low on his thigh. He was tall, but so were many in this country, and unless a man was close enough to catch the brittle look in his eyes, and to see the clean, hard line of his jaw, he escaped any particular notice.

Cole Ranier was sheriff here—that much High-Card had learned before coming. In the small office alongside the jail he found the lawman sitting behind a battered oak desk, wearing his five-pointed star at the left pocket of his faded tan shirt. Ranier looked up at High-Card's entrance, gave him a polite nod, and waited for him to state his business.

"I started the day your letter came," High-Card announced.

Ranier's frank brown eyes widened a trifle in surprise, and it was a full three seconds before he muttered: "Then you must be Stevens. You didn't waste much time." He fixed High-Card with an appraising glance that missed nothing, then, evidently satisfied with what he saw, leaned forward and spit deliberately into the woodbox beside his desk. He wiped his tobacco-stained mustache with the back of one hand and added: "I shouldn't have written that letter."

His statement brought little change in the face of his listener. High-Card waited in silence until at length Ranier sighed and explained: "When a man gets as old as I am, he has no business buyin' trouble. That's what I did when I wrote you."

"You were Jeff McBride's friend," High-Card reminded him. "So was I. Wasn't that reason enough for lettin' me know?"

"That's the way I looked at it first," the lawman agreed. "But there's more than the killin' of a friend in back of this."

High-Card shook his head and said impatiently: "Tell me who killed Jeff. I'll finish what I came for and ride away."

"Maybe you will and maybe you won't," Ranier said. Then, as High-Card was about to protest, the sheriff questioned: "Does the name Easterling mean anything to you?"

High-Card's eyes narrowed at the mention of that name, and his impatience of a moment ago was forgotten. "Easterling? There was a gent wearin' that handle who pulled Jeff out of a sinkhole in the Arkansas River years ago. We were takin' a trail herd north that year. Jeff would have been there yet if this Easterling hadn't thrown him a rope."

"Jeff thought you'd remember," Ranier said. "Abe Easterling lived here. He died two years ago, leavin' the biggest outfit on this range to his son and daughter. The girl, Judith, is a chip off the old block, as fine as they come, but the boy's a stray. The only thing he likes better than whiskey is a deck o' cards. In the last few weeks Bill Easterling has gambled away all the money his old man left him, and part of the girl's. Jeff was tryin' to stop that when he was cut down."

Ranier paused. High-Card waited a moment, then drawled: "Let's have the rest of it."

"There's a forked tinhorn in the saloon across the street by the name of Watt Avery. Jeff caught him usin' a marked deck against Bill Easterling one night. He called him on it, and Avery flipped a Derringer out of his coat sleeve and let Jeff have both barrels. I got to Jeff before he died and he asked me to get you down here. He said you'd know what to do."

High-Card's face had gone taut and pale. "That

shouldn't be hard," he breathed, "Where do I find Avery?"

"It won't be hard to find him," Ranier said. "But he works for Les Hammer. Hammer owns the saloon across there. This is Les Hammer's town."

"And you're Hammer's man?" High-Card queried.

Strangely enough, Ranier took no offense at the blunt words. He smiled thinly and said: "Some claim I am, but that's not the truth. I need this job and the best way o' keepin' it is to stay out of Hammer's way."

High-Card nodded soberly. He half turned and looked out the door toward the saloon awning opposite, muttering: "And what if the tinhorn and his forked deck don't last?"

"Tinhorns come cheap, Stevens."

High-Card glanced back over his shoulder at the lawman.

"What I've been workin' around to," Ranier explained, "is that Les Hammer wants the Lazy E, Easterling's outfit. And he'll get it, one way or another."

"I see," High-Card muttered, facing the door once more and studying the saloon across the street as though in this way he could find the answer to the many questions he was turning over in his mind. For eight days he had ridden with a burning hate eating into him—hatred for the man who had killed his friend. But now, within

14

reach of Jeff McBride's murderer, he was faced with the realization that more than the killing of a man was involved here.

High-Card could remember the evening, nearly eight years ago, when Abe Easterling had ridden into that lonely trail camp with the loose bulk of the man he had saved lying across his horse's withers—a Jeff more dead than alive from five tortuous hours of struggle against the quicksand of the Arkansas. Easterling had ridden away from the camp that night after they had revived Jeff, and that was the last High-Card had seen or heard of the man until now. He and Jeff had often spoken of him and Jeff had never forgotten the debt he owed him.

Thinking of this, High-Card idly watched a man shoulder his way out through the swing doors of the saloon opposite and saunter over to lean indolently against the adobe wall of the building. Suddenly all his thoughts were crowded into the background as he looked more closely. The man was outfitted in a sweeping black frock coat and wore a white shirt and a string tie. A flat-crowned black Stetson completed the gambler's rig, and the next instant High-Card was asking Ranier: "Is that the tinhorn across there?"

He turned to flash a glance back at the lawman and catch his answering nod. With that he forgot all but the galling hatred that had burned within him for the past eight days. He went out through the door and across the walk, ignoring the warning Ranier called out after him: "Remember that I'm the law here, Stevens! I'll have to come after you if you do this!"

Halfway across the dusty street High-Card slowed his pace as a girl came down the walk and approached the gambler. He saw Avery reach up to touch the brim of his hat in casual greeting. Then the girl was speaking, and High-Card was close enough to hear her say: "But I can't let it happen again! Bill lost more than a thousand dollars last night, and, if it goes on, there won't be a thing left!"

"I'm sorry, miss," came Avery's answer, "but I'm hired to deal to anyone who chooses to sit at my table."

The girl's glance measured him coldly for an instant, and then, wordless, she turned from him and went on down the street.

High-Card was all at once keenly aware of the striking freshness of her oval face, and of the deep richness of her chestnut hair and brown eyes, and then, knowing that this must be Judith Easterling, he put her from his mind and centered his attention once more on the gambler. The intensity of his look seemed to telegraph a warning to Avery, for at that moment the gambler's head jerked up and he looked across at High-Card and let his hands settle at his sides with the instinctive wariness of a man long accustomed to recognizing trouble.

High-Card stepped up to the walk in front of the gambler and said quietly: "They tell me you're the one who cut down on Jeff McBride."

The thin line of the gambler's mouth came down in the hint of a sneer. "And what if I am?"

"I sided Jeff for six years," High-Card drawled. "You can fill your hand any time."

He hadn't looked for it to happen so suddenly. One moment Avery was lazily pushing his spare frame out from his slouch against the wall, the next his two hands were suddenly clawed and sweeping his coat aside in a streaking draw. Never had High-Card's flat muscles moved with such speed and precision. Before his thought willed the action, his hand palmed out the heavy Colt and rocked it steady. As Avery's .45 swiveled up at him, he let his thumb slip off the hammer and took up the slamming whip of the weapon with a springy wrist that brought it back into line again as the roar of the gunshot ripped down the corridor of the street. With the thunder of that single explosion the gambler's frame rocked back against the wall. His upswinging gun faltered and fell from his hand, and into his eyes shot a gleam of incredible fury. But the look died an instant later to a vacant stare as his knees gave way and he fell forward. He was dead.

Quickly High-Card considered his chances.

17

There was yet time to get into his saddle and ride out of here. But he was remembering Judith Easterling, remembering, too, Ranier's words: "Tinhorns come cheap!"

A sudden decision made him step around the dead man and put the adobe wall of the saloon at his back. He heard shouts and saw people running toward him along the walk nearby. They slowed and kept their distance, however, as they saw the smoking six-gun in his hand.

He glanced around warily, searching the faces of those closest for any sign of hostility. Twenty feet away, down the walk, stood Judith Easterling. Her eyes were wide with horror.

Cole Ranier ran out of his office and came across the street with a stiffly awkward stride. He pushed in through the loosely forming circle and stood in front of High-Card. With a single, cursory glance down at the dead man, he looked over at High-Card and said flatly: "You should have made your getaway, stranger. Now I'll have to ask you for your cutter."

On the heel of his words a thick-set man outfitted in expensive boots and broadcloth trousers and an immaculately laundered white shirt shouldered roughly through the crowd from the direction of the saloon entrance. Ranier looked at him and the line of his mouth tightened.

"I'm arrestin' him, Hammer," the lawman said briefly.

"Think again," High-Card put in coldly, lining his gun on the sheriff. "This jasper went for his iron first. That makes it self-defense. There'll be no arrest, tin star!"

Ranier's gaunt face flushed under the derisive words, but, staring intently at the lawman, High-Card managed to convey a hint of the play he was making. Then he looked at Les Hammer in time to see the saloon owner's black eyes whip up from the dead man and fix steadily on him. Hammer measured him calmly for the space of seconds, then reached up to take the short stub of a chewed cigar from his mouth and say gruffly: "What did you hold against Avery, stranger?"

"He made the mistake of usin' a five-ace deck against a gambler down in Bisbee a year or so ago," High-Card lied.

"Who was this gambler?" The saloon owner's eyes were narrow-lidded as he put the question.

In answer, High-Card tapped his chest with a curved forefinger. The gesture made Hammer's thick brows contract in a frown, and his look gradually took on a shade of interest. His eyes ran down to examine High-Card's leveled weapon and his long, tapering fingers.

Turning to Ranier he said: "Let it go, Cole. Avery's been on the prod for this. I reckon it was his fault." He looked up at High-Card once more and added: "This leaves a table open in my place, stranger. Will you take a job?"

High-Card shook his head. "I don't bank the tank towns, friend!" He lowered his .45 and dropped it into his holster. "I'm ridin' straight through."

Hammer's face flushed in quick anger at this unlooked for arrogance. Yet he checked his feeling and turned away to push out through the crowd, calling back to the sheriff: "I'll pay for the box and the preachin', Cole! Do the funeral up right!"

Ranier was plainly bewildered at the outcome of the affair, yet he gave no sign of recognition as he looked across at this apparent stranger. But as High-Card edged away through the circle that surrounded the dead man, the lawman recovered composure enough to voice a warning: "Go easy on the gun play, stranger. You won't be so lucky a second time."

High-Card sauntered on up the walk, glad to be away from the crowd. The thing he had come here to do was finished. Yet, as it turned out, it was now strangely unsatisfying to realize that he had avenged Jeff McBride's death. His thoughts centered on Les Hammer's offer. The saloon owner needed another gambler and would waste no time in hiring one. Avery's death would make little difference in the state of Judith Easterling's concern. Hammer, having set out to own the Lazy E, would not stop now. Thinking of the girl, he was surprised to hear a light, quick step on the walk behind him, and to turn and see that she had followed him away from the crowd.

"Wait," she said breathlessly. And when he had slowed his stride so that she stood beside him: "I . . . I want to thank you for what you've done. You can't know what this means to me."

"I do know," High-Card told her. "But what has happened won't make any difference."

"Then you know . . . you know about Bill?" she queried.

High-Card nodded.

The girl sighed wearily, something of her high spirits all at once deserting her. "I'll try again," she began lamely. "I'll try to keep Bill away from there. If it goes on, we're lost." She paused a moment, getting a hold on her emotions before she went on: "It's strange to be thanking one man for killing another. But I do thank you."

An idea was crying for recognition in High-Card's mind. At first he put it aside, then suddenly he felt a rising wonder at the logic of the thing. Almost before he had reasoned it through, he heard himself saying: "You'd better not be seen talking to me. There's something I can do about this. Your brother is safe."

Before she had the chance to question him, he brushed on past her and walked down the street. Yet he had one fleeting glimpse of the gratitude that lighted her eyes. Sight of it made him uncertain again. He had promised her a lot.

21

II

High-Card waited until mid-afternoon, when the single street of Gunflash lay nearly deserted under the glaring heat of the early autumn sun. Then he made his way into the Mother Lode Saloon and stepped to the deserted bar and ordered a straight bourbon. A single glance around the room showed him only three other occupants grouped around a poker table at the rear.

The barkeep put out a bottle and glass and, picking up a towel, started polishing glassware on the back counter. As he worked, he whistled tunelessly. As though this whistling was a pre-arranged signal, a door at the back end of the bar opened and Les Hammer stepped out of his office. He looked along the bar, raised his brows in surprise at sight of High-Card, and stepped around the end of the counter and strolled toward him.

"The offer still holds, stranger," he said, as he stopped alongside High-Card.

"So does my answer."

Hammer shrugged his broad shoulders in unconcern and poured himself a drink, downing it at a gulp. Then he remarked casually: "There's something in my office I'd like to show you."

Before High-Card could make a reply, the saloon owner turned and walked the length of

22

the bar and reëntered his office. High-Card masked his curiosity and followed, stepping in and closing the door behind him as Hammer took the swivel chair behind his polished mahogany desk.

"It won't do you any good," High-Card offered as the latch clicked shut behind him. "I quit playin' penny-ante before I started shavin'."

Hammer disregarded the remark, although a faintly amused look came to his eyes. Without answering, he wheeled around in his chair to face a small safe that stood at the back wall of the room. He leaned over and spun the dial, and in a few seconds the heavy door swung open. Reaching in, Hammer lifted out a thick bundle of banknotes and tossed them upon the desk.

"There's Watt Avery's roll, stranger. He came here broke less than three weeks ago. There's four thousand dollars lyin' there. You can't call that tank-town coin."

"Did he run onto a sucker?" High-Card drawled, letting a shade of interest show in his tone.

Hammer smiled, but instead of answering he said: "You could earn this money. More, if you want. That puts it up to you. Will you take the job?"

"What kind of a job?"

"You'll take over my back table as dealer for a week, no questions asked."

High-Card shook his head. "No. If there's a

forked play, I'll either be in on it all the way, or not at all. I'm headed for Tombstone, Hammer. It doesn't matter to me where I build my roll."

Hammer's coarse face was set inscrutably. Even so, he betrayed a measure of his anxiety. He focused on High-Card a glance as cold as chilled steel, but when High-Card met it unflinchingly, the look softened a trifle. Then, almost affably, Hammer offered: "I'll tell you this much. There's a jasper here with more money than sense. He's droppin' a thousand or two every night. Avery used marked cards. Maybe you won't have to. But I want this gent broke within a week. He owns a ranch. It's the ranch I want, not the money. Is that plain enough?"

"What's my take?" High-Card asked.

"An even split with the house. Work it any way you want, only break him! And the sooner the better!"

"I play it my own way?"

Hammer nodded.

"Then you've hired yourself a dealer," was High-Card's level answer. "Tell me about this sucker."

At nine o'clock that night, Les Hammer sauntered back to face his new dealer from across the green felt rear table of his saloon. He caught High-Card's eye, and with a barely perceptible nod indicated a man at the bar. High-Card's glance

24

ran on past the saloon owner and singled out Bill Easterling.

Short and spare, Easterling wore a *concha* belt holding a tooled holster and ivory-handled six-gun. He had his sister's deep chestnut hair, but, as he turned and faced the rear of the room, High-Card saw that his light blue eyes were weak and red-rimmed from long days of a whiskey diet.

In less than twenty minutes Easterling made his way on back and stood beside the gaming table. He swayed a little as he reached into his pocket and lifted out a thick roll of greenbacks. Tossing them on the table, he grinned and said to the two players facing High-Card: "Move out, gents! I'm here for a cleanin'!"

His tone and manner sent a hot flood of anger coursing through High-Card who was about to voice a barbed retort when he realized that Easterling was inviting the very thing Hammer had hired him to do. So, as the other two sitting at the table rose from their chairs without protest and cashed in their chips on the low-stakes game, High-Card said in a level tone: "Name your game, stranger."

At the sound of High-Card's voice Easterling frowned and bent down so that his broad-brimmed Stetson shaded his eyes. He stared at High-Card, his frown deepening, and said thickly: "You're new here. Where's Watt Avery?"

"He cashed in and left town this afternoon,"

High-Card answered. "What stakes are you namin'?"

Easterling straightened up and gave a careless shrug of his thin shoulders before he eased into the chair across the table. "Make it stud at a ten-dollar limit," he muttered, licking his thumb and forefinger and counting out $500 in paper money. "I feel lucky tonight. A new dealer and new cards! Gather round, gents, and watch the fun!"

Several men had followed him away from the bar. These now ringed the table, along with the two players who had vacated their seats a moment ago. High-Card realized that most of these men had come here for the express purpose of watching Bill Easterling try his luck against the house. Word had made the rounds that Hammer had hired a new tinhorn, and the crowd was expecting big things.

Play commenced, with High-Card using an unmarked deck. For the first half hour the difference between the two players was little. But during that half hour High-Card learned that Bill Easterling knew a lot about poker. The man played a steady game, rarely bluffing and betting his cards only when he had them. This, then, was clear proof of Hammer's claim that Easterling had been cheated out of his money.

At the end of an hour Easterling was $240 the winner. He was in high spirits, and his winning streak prompted him to order a bottle of whiskey.

He placed the bottle at his elbow and took an occasional drink from it. As the whiskey worked in him, his perceptions seemed to become sharper than before. Luck was with him, and in a run of good hands he cleaned up another $100.

High-Card had thought through his plan that afternoon, after talking with Hammer, and Easterling's run of luck helped along his plan. Now, with his opponent taking more than his share of the heavy pots, High-Card began throwing away winning hands. Once he refused to call three kings with a full house. Another time he let Easterling take a $90 pot with a straight against a flush.

It was at this point that High-Card looked up to see Les Hammer standing behind Easterling. Others had seen the saloon owner come up, and now they backed away and gave him room. There was a long half minute in which an utter silence cloaked the saloon, for it was obvious from the frown on Hammer's face and the way he was chewing his cigar that he was dissatisfied with the way High-Card's luck was running. He caught High-Card's eye and nodded his head signifi-cantly in the direction of his office before he turned and left the table.

At the finish of that hand, High-Card announced: "Time out for drinks, pardner. We'll go at it again in ten minutes." He paid Easterling for the chips stacked in front of him, and then rose from the table and went to the bar for a drink. Behind him a sudden hum of excited conversation broke loose. As soon as the group around the table had broken up and drifted to the bar, High-Card went on back to Hammer's office.

The saloon owner's thick-set bulk sat rigidly erect in the swivel chair behind the desk as High-Card entered and closed the door behind him. Hammer's cold stare measured him for the space of five seconds, and then he said flatly: "I hired you to break Easterling. Maybe you didn't understand."

High-Card threw one leg over the near corner of the desk and sat facing Hammer. There was an amused glint behind his gray eyes, and he waited until he had lifted a tobacco sack out of his shirt pocket before he made his reply. "I haven't forgotten," he said calmly. "I'll need another two thousand to run out his luck."

Hammer lunged up out of his chair, his two fists planted on the desk top. "You want another two thousand?" he repeated menacingly. "Can't you hand him three . . . or four? Let's have it! What's the play?"

"To let Easterling win tonight. To let him win a lot."

"But, blast it, he's not to win! I told you I . . . ."

"You want me to break him," High-Card interrupted in his slow drawl. He was smiling openly now as he flicked alight a match and touched it to the end of his cigarette. "Don't forget our deal, Hammer. I was to do this my own way. I'll need two thousand more . . . tonight."

A puzzled frown erased some of the wrath from Hammer's face. Abruptly he eased back into his chair and said: "Go on, tinhorn. Either you're a bloody fool, or you have more brains than I've ever hired before."

"Easterling wins tonight," explained High-Card. "He wins plenty . . . three thousand or better, if I can rig it without giving it away. Tomorrow night he comes back for more. He wins a little, not much. The next night I prime him to come back for a killin'. And that night I'll clean him." High-Card paused, letting his words take effect. Then: "I told you I never played at penny ante, Hammer."

A crooked smile wreathed Les Hammer's face. That smile gave way to a chuckle, and then the chuckle became a barely audible laugh that shook the man's burly frame. "And I thought Watt Avery and his marked deck was the only way!" he cried. "Brother, you and me could take over this town. Do this any way you choose." He reached into his hip pocket and, bringing out a wallet, counted out $2,000 in paper money. Pushing it across the desk to High-Card, he said affably: "Take it. And if you need more, there's plenty where this came from."

• • •

Race Tipton, the saddle tramp, was one of the watchers alongside the poker layout when Bill Easterling cashed in that night at 12:30, $2,780 the winner. Race Tipton knew cards and couldn't understand drunken Bill Easterling's luck against High-Card, a man he recognized as a professional gambler.

His curiosity aroused, Tipton kept his eyes open. Later, when Easterling left for the livery barn after a round of drinks with a few of his admiring friends, Tipton went out front and leaned inconspicuously against a corner of the saloon, keeping his eyes open. A few minutes afterward, he saw High-Card leave the saloon and head for the hotel. When Judith Easterling stepped out from the shadows of the awning in front of the building alongside the hotel to stop High-Card, Tipton saw and recognized her and wondered.

High-Card was saying to the girl: "You shouldn't have met me here tonight. Bill's on his way home with three thousand dollars. Tomorrow night I'll fix it so that he wins again. After that, I can't make any promises."

Tipton, across the street, didn't hear that. But a half minute later, when the girl stepped back out of sight and High-Card went on into the hotel, Tipton went back into the saloon and along the bar to knock on the door of Les Hammer's office.

When he heard Hammer's gruff voice sound inside, he opened the door and went in.

Hammer looked across at him and growled impatiently: "So you're back again?"

Tipton was old, bent by years in the saddle, and he had a weak chin and shifty blue eyes that couldn't meet Hammer's direct stare. His manner was strangely meek, for he stood with his Stetson in his hands and shifted his feet nervously.

While the fellow was trying to summon an answer, Hammer said: "I told you to get out of the country. I don't aim to have a tramp like you seen too much around my place. What did you do with the double eagle I gave you yesterday?"

Tipton lifted his shoulders in a shrug, and for a moment let a hint of pride show in his eyes as he said in a half snarl: "How far can a man get on that kind of money?" Then, seeing the quick anger that flared in Hammer's eyes, he held up a protesting hand and went on, hurriedly: "Now wait, boss! You'll be glad I didn't go. I've found out somethin' that should be worth money to you . . . enough money to tide me over until I can work over into the next state."

"Be quick about it, Race. You know damn' well what I do with an understrapper that tries a double-cross. What if I go over and tell Ranier what I know?"

"Boss, I swear I'm doin' you a right turn this time. It's about this new dealer you hired today. Him and Bill Easterling . . ."

Hammer chuckled, his good humor revived by

31

the mention of High-Card's name. For the past twenty minutes Les Hammer had lost himself in greedy visions of what he and High-Card could do after they were finished with this Easterling. Why, they might wind up by owning the whole town. And now, to realize that Race Tipton somehow suspected what was going on—well, strangely enough it amused him. He lifted a hand and waved the oldster to silence: "I know all about that. It's a frame-up. Two nights from now Bill Easterling won't own his own saddle." He reached into his pocket and took out two double eagles and tossed them across so that they fell at Race Tipton's feet. "Don't say I'm not generous, Race. Now get the devil out and let me alone!"

Tipton was about to ask the saloon owner if he knew that his forked dealer had been talking with Judith Easterling, but he bit back the words in time, picked up the money, and went out. Inside him burned a vicious hatred for Les Hammer, who kept him drunk so he could use him, and was now throwing him aside like a worn-out boot.

He slept in an abandoned lean-to along the alley that night. No, he wasn't leaving the country. He'd keep an eye on this new dealer of Hammer's, and, when the time came to cash in on what he knew—what Hammer couldn't know—he'd ride away from here with enough gold in his pocket to see him across two states and down into Mexico.

III

The next night, Bill Easterling appeared at the back table of the Mother Lode at nine, drunk, his eyes red-rimmed and his speech thick. High-Card, finishing a deal, smiled and said to the two players who sat at the table: "Give up your seats, gentle-men, and watch the fun."

The pair had been waiting for this, and gladly cashed in and made way for the big game of the evening. Easterling, as he sat down, glared across at High-Card and nodded to a red-headed cow-puncher who stood behind him, saying thickly: "I think I can beat you, stranger. But just to be sure it's a straight game, I've brought Red along to watch you."

No man before Bill Easterling had ever spoken to High-Card Stevens in such a manner and lived to tell about it. But tonight, with the stakes higher than any that would show on the table, High-Card checked the impulse to reach for his gun and his smile held as he drawled: "Have Red take a chair. This will be a straight game, Easterling."

Easterling was still frowning as he reached into a back pocket of his Levi's and took out two fresh, unopened packs of cards. He threw them on the table, saying: "We'll use these."

"Suit yourself."

High-Card picked up one deck and, breaking it open, began the deal, straight stud at the $10 limit of last night. Ten minutes after the game began High-Card had to ask the crowd to move back a little from the table. At least fifty men were watching, and chairs were selling at a dollar apiece so that those in back could stand on them to see the play. The bar was deserted.

Les Hammer looked on for the first few minutes, chewing his cigar and smiling in satisfaction as he saw the way High-Card was playing it tonight. High-Card was winning those first hands, and Bill Easterling wasn't liking it.

At length, Hammer went on across to his office. Shortly after he had left, Race Tipton walked in through the swing doors up front and looked furtively at the office door. Then he edged into the crowd surrounding the table and in ten minutes had made his way through to the inner circle, leaning against the back wall. From here he had an occasional glimpse of High-Card's hand, for High-Card was sitting with his back to the wall.

A tenseness held the crowd as High-Card's luck began to change. Aside from the sudden hum of conversation at the outcome of a particularly close hand, these watchers were as quiet as though attending a funeral.

Easterling's chip stacks grew in size. He was even, then ahead of the game. Then he lost his run of luck for a stretch, regained it, and shortly after 10:00 was $400 the winner.

At eleven, after he'd lost $1,000, High-Card went to Hammer's office. The greeting the saloon owner gave him was a different one than he had received on the previous night, however. When High-Card asked for the loan of the dead Watt Avery's $4,000 roll, Hammer gladly opened the safe and handed it over.

When play resumed, Race Tipton was standing even closer to High-Card. He was an unobtrusive sort of person, however, and High-Card, intent on his game, paid the oldster little attention. In the next two hours, with never a let-up in the game, Bill Easterling won close to $2,000. It was done nicely, too, for the winning sobered Bill a little and he played a clean, heady game.

Once he said: "I'm likin' this, tinhorn. You and me'll have to sit down here often."

The crowd was with Easterling tonight, for drunk or sober, there was not a man there that didn't realize what this would mean to Bill and his sister. They took in High-Card's apparent discomfort and gloried in the fact that the house was taking a trimming.

It was over at 1:30.

Easterling looked across at High-Card and said: "You've had enough."

High-Card nodded and pretended concern. "I know it, brother," he said dully. "I'll pay you five hundred a night to stay away from this table."

"The devil you will. Tomorrow night, the same time. And you'll either deal with me, or I'll have the law close this layout."

When Easterling got out of his chair, slapped his partner, Red, on the back, and got ready to leave, Les Hammer was there to put in his word. The saloon owner looked worried and said: "This about evens us up, Bill. Maybe you ought to lay off for a spell."

Easterling straightened from his slouch, and for a moment High-Card, looking on, thought he saw a hint of strength creep into the man's eyes. "Hammer," said Easterling, "you've called the deal and now you'll back your play."

Hammer shrugged and, chewing on his cigar, left the circle of onlookers. After Easterling had gone, High-Card went to the office. As he closed the door behind him, Hammer began laughing. He laughed until the tears came to his eyes.

"Brother, you're the slickest article that ever hit this town! He thinks he's all set to clean me out of every dollar in my safe. Did I hold up my end out there a minute ago?"

"That was nice." High-Card grinned. "Tomorrow night we start the killin'. It's got me worn-out. I think I'll turn in."

High-Card left the saloon and walked down to the hotel. On the way, he saw Easterling and a half dozen others sauntering toward the livery barn.

These were the men who had celebrated the hardest over Bill's winnings. They were drunk, to a man, laughing and shouting, and one or two trying to sing. High-Card recognized one of them particularly as the quiet oldster who had stood alongside the table during most of the play that night.

This was Race Tipton. He didn't belong where he was, among Bill Easterling's friends, and sober they wouldn't have had him around. But he was being a good fellow tonight and no one resented his presence.

Bill was riding a strange horse home, leaving his bay in town for a set of new shoes at the blacksmith's. Someone picked a salty palomino for Bill, and Tipton was there to help saddle. He even gave Bill a hand into the saddle. The light in the stable wasn't strong, and Bill Easterling's senses had been blunted by the liquor he had drunk. So Easterling didn't feel the practiced darting of Race Tipton's hand as it snaked in and out of the right-hand pocket of his Levi's.

Race's hand was barely big enough to close on that bundle of banknotes. It was a clumsy job, but he managed to get the money into his pocket without being seen. Then he stood with the rest and watched Bill and Red Armstrong start off down the street, headed out the east trail for home.

• • •

Two minutes later Race was entering Les Hammer's office, this time without knocking. He went straight to Hammer's desk, leaned against it, and said: "Les, you're gettin' the double-cross as strong as it ever came!"

Hammer took the cigar out of his mouth and drawled flatly: "I thought I told you to hit the high lonesome, friend Race. Maybe I still ought to tell Ranier what I know."

But Tipton wasn't listening. All his meekness was gone now, and with a confident gesture he reached into his pocket and took out the loosely folded sheaf of banknotes he had lifted out of Bill Easterling's pocket.

Hammer looked and asked: "What's that?"

"Easterling's!"

Hammer held out a hand and said sharply: "So you're up to the old tricks! Hand it over!"

Race threw the money on the desk. "Let it lay, Les . . . until you've heard what I have to say."

"Go on."

"I need that money, and I'll trade it for what I know. Is it a deal?"

Hammer was drawing on his cigar again, a trifle stunned at the arrogance of a man he had always thought weak. Finally he said: "Spill what you know and I'll decide."

"Last night I saw your fake tinhorn talkin' to

Judith Easterling . . . after her brother had cleaned you out of three thousand."

For a full five seconds Les Hammer sat motionlessly in his chair. Then his big frame became taut, the color drained from his face, and his eyes took on a hard, brittle light. At length, he breathed hoarsely: "Take that money, Race. Get out of the country and don't ever let me see you again."

Race pocketed the money once more, saying confidently: "In case it'll help you, Easterling isn't ridin' his own jughead tonight. He's forkin' a palomino from the livery barn. I thought maybe . . ."

"Get out!"

The oldster clamped his jaw shut and his sureness left him. When he stepped backward through the door, awed by the menace in Hammer's voice, he was once more his old meek self. Outside, he didn't stop long. He went to the livery stable at a half run, paid his bill, and climbed into his saddle to take the road west out of town, riding hard.

Les Hammer's black look didn't change for a full two minutes after Race Tipton had gone. But when it did, it was replaced by one of such incredible cunning that a strong man, seeing him, would have felt his blood run cold. He was remembering that parting remark of Race's—the one about Easterling's riding the palomino.

Hammer took a gun—a long-barreled .38 Colt—out of his safe and rammed it into the pocket of his coat. Then, taking down his Stetson and jamming it upon his head, he blew out the office lamp and left by the back door.

He walked the length of the alley, then east. At the very limits of the town he strode up to a small shed and, opening the door, went in. Lighting a lantern, he quickly saddled a roan gelding that stood in the single stall. In two minutes he was riding south, at right angles to the trail to the east that Bill Easterling and Red would be taking on their ride home.

IV

Hammer rode for an hour, swinging east after two miles of steady going. At the end of that hour, he dismounted and flattened himself on the rock ledge of an outcropping a dozen feet above the faint line of a trail. He had staked his roan a good 100 yards in back of the outcropping, in a thick growth of cedars. Now, with his Colt resting lightly in his palm, his hearing attuned to all the sounds of the night, he waited.

He had a long wait. That last round of drinks in the Mother Lode had nearly finished Bill Easterling. Twenty minutes ago, two miles from town, the palomino had pitched Bill's loose bulk out of the saddle. Red Armstrong, knowing what a time his friend would have riding a half-broken colt for ten miles, had picked Bill up and said: "You need a rockin' chair tonight, Bill. Change onto my jughead."

Easterling didn't mind. He was singing now, and didn't even pause in his off-key tune as Red helped him to his feet and into Red's saddle. From then on the going was better, Red managing the palomino easily and even lending his baritone voice to the rendition of "Red River Valley." They were halfway through the tenth chorus when they pulled even with the outcropping.

Suddenly the deafening blast of Les Hammer's .38 chopped in on the high note and Red Armstrong felt a sudden searing pain along his ribs. The palomino reared and pitched him. Falling, he lit heavily on one shoulder and his head snapped back and hit the ground, hard. The blow set a blaze of white light dancing before Red's eyes, and gradually his senses faded.

Les Hammer waited for only two seconds— long enough to see dimly in the darkness that the rider of the palomino was down and lying motionlessly. Then, before the second rider up ahead could turn and come back, Hammer tumbled down off the high finger of rock and ran as fast as his legs would carry him.

Behind, he heard a wild shouting and the *thud* of the palomino's hoofs as the animal cut back along the trail for town. By the time the second rider, Red Armstrong as Hammer thought, had cut around the outcropping, Hammer was already in the saddle of his roan and riding rapidly away.

It had worked out better than he had planned. All that remained was a hard ride back to town, to get there before the palomino showed up at the livery stable.

Hammer made the ten miles in forty minutes, walking the road silently up to the shed and stabling his horse in the darkness. He even remembered to rub down the horse. Then, hearing a trotting horse coming in along the trail, he left the shed and took to the alley, passing the rear of the hotel and going on to the saloon.

In his office once more, he opened the safe and took out a money box. Out of the box he counted a trifle more than $3,000 in well-used, dog-eared banknotes. Bill Easterling had won that much tonight.

High-Card tossed restlessly on his bed, unable to sleep after the nerve-racking hours he had spent facing Bill Easterling at the poker layout. Nor could he put from his mind the look Judith Easterling had given him last night as she stood there talking with him in the shadow of the street awning. It was the look a woman gives the man of her choice, yet even now High-Card could not believe he had read it right. It prompted disturbing thoughts—thoughts that led to wild imaginings he knew would never be reality. All the bitterness of his lonesome years crowded up to taunt him now. A girl like Judith Easterling was not for his kind.

Finally, to ease the tautness of his nerves, he climbed from his bed and took his tobacco from the pocket of his shirt, which was hanging from the foot of the bed. Then he went on to the window to build a cigarette. The glow of a late-rising moon afforded him sufficient light to sift the tobacco upon the rice paper and roll it into a tight cylinder. As he was reaching down to the sill to scratch a match, his eyes dropped to the alley below. Then, at the far limits of his vision, he thought he caught a hint of movement. The hand holding the match went taut, and he turned his head to look down the alley. There, edging along beneath the shadows of the outbuildings, he made out the thick-set figure of Les Hammer.

An instant alarm coursed through him. Where had Hammer been this late at night, and what made him want to hide his presence by walking down an alley? Rapidly High-Card ran back over the night's happenings. As quickly as it had come, his alarm subsided. It was impossible that Hammer's presence out there could have anything to do with his own affairs. Strangely enough, the incident seemed to ease his mind and he tossed his shirt and unlighted cigarette upon a chair and went back to bed. In two minutes he was asleep.

Short minutes later the loud crash of a gun butt on the panel of his door jerked High-Card into abrupt wakefulness. He was pushing himself up in bed, reaching for the gun that hung from the bed post, as the door swung open and Les Hammer stepped into the room with a .45 lined in his blunt fist.

"Forget that gun!" Hammer barked out, motioning with his own weapon for High-Card to raise his hands.

As High-Card obeyed the unspoken command, Hammer stepped aside, and Sheriff Ranier entered the room. The lawman's face was grim and his eyes held no hint of the softness High-Card had seen in them before.

Before High-Card had a chance to speak, Ranier was saying: "We'll take a look at your things, Stevens. Better sit there quiet and take things easy. Hammer has it in his head you did it."

"Did what?" High-Card queried tonelessly.

"Bill Easterling's been killed. Or so Hammer thinks. The palomino Easterling took out tonight just drifted into the barn, luggin' a saddle with some blood on it. I've sent a deputy out the trail to have a look."

"But why me?"

Ranier looked at Hammer and said: "You tell him, Les."

"After you lost that money to Easterling last night, you asked for another chance at him,"

Hammer said. "I told you it'd have to be with your own money. You agreed. Tonight you lost three thousand to Easterling . . . your money this time. I say you followed Easterling out on the trail and dry-gulched him."

This deliberate lie set a coolness running along High-Card's nerves—a wariness that warned him to be careful. There was no use denying what Hammer said, for he was a stranger to Ranier and Hammer would have his way with his hired lawman. So he watched carefully for a chance as Ranier stepped to the bed and reached across for the gun hanging from the bed post. As the lawman moved, Hammer stepped in close to the front of the bed and, kneeling down, reached under to pull out High-Card's slicker roll. Before Ranier could move to see what he was doing, Hammer had the straps off the slicker and had unfolded it.

When Ranier looked over the foot of the bed, it was to see a wadded pile of banknotes lying in a fold of the slicker. Without bothering to examine the money closely, Ranier said soberly: "You win, Hammer. Stevens, you might have hid it better, knowin' we'd find Bill sooner or later."

High-Card slipped out of bed and reached for his shirt, which was lying on a chair near his pillow. He was picking it up, when steps sounded in the hallway outside.

Ranier and High-Card looked toward the open door. All at once Bill Easterling stepped through the opening. Here was a different Bill Easterling than the one High-Card knew. He walked steadily, and his eyes were no longer weak-looking. He looked from Ranier to High-Card, then to Hammer.

Hammer hadn't taken his eyes off High-Card, so that he didn't see who stood behind him.

Easterling said: "What's the trouble, Sheriff?"

With the sound of that voice—the voice of a man he had thought dead—Les Hammer wheeled swiftly to face the door, gun leveled.

At the same instant High-Card threw his shirt at Hammer's head. Startled and half blinded, Hammer thumbed his weapon and sent one wild shot lancing toward the door.

Easterling's hand stabbed toward his holstered .45. Ranier, amazed at what he saw, felt a tug at his holster and whirled to find his gun in High-Card's hand.

Hammer clawed the shirt from his face and stepped back so that he faced High-Card. The weapons of the two men swiveled into line in unison, and both blasted away the silence at the same split second. High-Card winced as Hammer's bullet tore into the thick muscle at his thigh, but his own bullet had sent the saloon owner staggering backward.

Hammer wasn't down, however. He leaned back against the wall, and, with a gleam of incredible fury flashing from his black eyes, he leveled his gun again and thumbed the hammer. High-Card dodged to one side, away from Ranier, his wrist taking the jarring buck of his gun as he lined it and pulled the trigger three times in quick succession. He saw Hammer's white shirt ripple as the bullets took him in the chest, and each hole in the cloth was ringed by a smear of blood. But still Hammer stayed on his feet, throwing his shots wildly.

High-Card's weapon now *clicked* hollowly as the hammer fell on an empty chamber. He savagely threw the gun aside, helpless for one brief instant. In that interval Les Hammer's shrill, mad laugh echoed through the room. A desperate, dying strength was keeping the man on his feet. He lifted his arm and aimed his .38 just as High-Card left his feet in a rolling lunge that took him across the bed.

Hammer never fired that gun again. Bill Easterling had been waiting there at the door for his chance, and he had it now. He took careful aim and once more a bullet blast beat outward at the walls. A blue hole centered Hammer's left temple. With instant death loosening his muscles, he slid to the floor and rolled upon his back, staring with glassy eyes at the ceiling.

As High-Card stepped across to look down at Hammer, Ranier said: "Then it was him, after all?"

High-Card shrugged his shoulders, and it was Easterling who answered the lawman's question. "I know a few things now, Ranier," he said. "For instance, I've found out about the slick little jasper that had his hand in my pocket when I climbed onto that palomino tonight."

Between the three of them they pieced together a fairly clear story. Easterling had stayed with Red Armstrong only long enough to learn that Red wasn't seriously hurt. Then he had ridden to town, sober, and had met Ranier's deputy and sent him to look after Red.

"The deputy also found Race Tipton," Easterling explained. "Race had gotten drunk on the money Hammer had given him and had fallen off his horse. Race confessed that he'd tipped off Hammer that I'd be riding home on a palomino, and said he was sure, from the way Hammer had acted, that Hammer'd go out and try to dry-gulch me."

Judith Easterling came up to the room a half hour later just as the medico had finished bandaging the wound in High-Card's thigh. She hadn't been able to explain Bill's absence and had ridden in to find out what was wrong.

Someone below had told her what had happened. She stepped inside and stood there a moment, looking across at High-Card. Then, choking back a sob, she crossed the room and knelt beside the bed and kissed him.

Bill Easterling saw something in his sister's eyes then, something that helped him to understand things a little better. His sister loved this tinhorn. Things weren't very straight to him yet, but Bill stepped over and pulled the girl to her feet. Then he took her in his arms and said humbly: "I reckon it's never too late to make a new start, Sis. Maybe we can forget what's happened."

"No," High-Card put in, looking up with a grin. "Because I'll always be around to see that you don't."

Unwanted Gold

Jonathan Hurff Glidden was born in Kewanee, Illinois and was graduated from the University of Illinois with a degree in English literature. In his career as a Western writer he published sixteen novels and over 120 short novels and short stories for the magazine market. His Peter Dawson novels are noted for their adept plotting, interesting and well-developed characters, their authentically researched historical backgrounds, and stylistic flair. The first Peter Dawson novel, THE CRIMSON HORSESHOE, won the Dodd, Mead Prize as the best Western of the year 1941 and ran serially in Street & Smith's *Western Story Magazine* prior to book publication. "Unwanted Gold" first appeared as "Gun Destiny of the Branded" in *Western Novel and Short Stories* (5/39). The author was paid $45. For its appearance here, both the author's original title and text have been restored.

I

Ned Olney, one of the house men, opened the door at the rear of the Nugget's dance floor and edged into the office. The closing of the door behind him effectively muted the din of the saloon—the off-key pound of the piano and the shuffle of many feet along the flimsy wooden floor directly outside, the *clink* of glasses and the fitful drone of loud talk and louder laughter sounding back from the bar. It was comparatively quiet in here.

Olney announced briefly: "There's a stranger cleanin' up at Table Three, Mike."

The man addressed as Mike sat beneath a high window in the wall, at a scarred deal desk six feet across the small cubbyhole room. His legs were thrust out toward a sheet-iron stove in the room's far corner. He was hawk-visaged, dark, and his broadcloth coat fit him tightly over heavily muscled shoulders. He glanced once at a girl sitting in a deep leather chair beyond a small box-like safe alongside the desk, then asked his house man: "How much?"

"Sixty-four hundred in five hands."

Mike's eyes went narrow-lidded in faint surprise. He took his cigar from a mouth that made a thin straight line below his evenly clipped black mustache. "That's enough," he said. "Get rid of him."

The girl in the chair straightened. She wore a white dress; her hair was taffy-colored, and her eyes the green of the silk that edged the ruffles of her full skirt. She was young and her face was strikingly pretty. Just now she looked at Mike with obvious puzzlement in her glance, and, when she spoke, there was a gentle reprimand in her tone. "Mike, I thought you were a gambler."

Mike shook his head. "I never buck a man's luck, Kit. Get rid of him, Ned."

"He doesn't look like he'd scare," Olney said dryly. "He's packin' an iron and my guess is he can use it."

Mike's glance traveled down to the pair of low-slung holsters riding beneath the tail of Olney's serge coat. "You ought to know, Ned. Better close the game on him then. Close all the games on him."

Olney left the room. He crossed the dance floor, weaving in and out among the percentage girls with their somber-outfitted partners, who were mostly miners in from the diggings to spend their day's pay. He shouldered through the tight-packed circle of onlookers surrounding Table Three, caught Bill Beeson's eye, and gave a meager shake of his head. He waited the half minute until the hand was finished, watching the stranger once more rake in the chips piled at the table's center, and then hearing Bill Beeson announce— "Game's closed for a few minutes, gentlemen." He made his way to the remaining poker tables and finally to the four faro layouts, telling each house man: "Shut down if that saddle bum works your way. Boss' orders."

Dave Sanders was no saddle bum, although he wore the outfit—Levi's, cotton shirt and open vest, Stetson and soft boots—that was the coin of all the range beyond these hills. He was a tall, flat-hipped cowpuncher whose footloose urge to ride beyond the far horizon had made him give up his job as top hand for one of the big outfits across the desert six days ago. A live curiosity to taste the life of this new boom camp of Aspen Gulch had drawn him here. He had bleached blond hair and a pair of smiling pale blue eyes and his lean face was sun-blackened to the color of new saddle leather.

He had been at first amused at having to pay $4 to feed and stable his tired roan tonight at the end of his ride, and he was more than amused when it cost him another $3 for a poor meal of two fried eggs, salt pork, stale bread, and coffee. And finally he was faintly angry to have to hand across $5 to the owner of the Mountain View, Aspen Gulch's one hotel, for the privilege of reserving a night's sleep on the graveyard shift, the hours from midnight to eight in the morning, on a cot in a room lined with ten other cots.

With four hours on his hands to wait out his turn to sleep, he had come down the crowded plank walk along the town's one muddy street and turned in here at the Nugget. A drink of raw bourbon had come to an even dollar. Then, leaning back against the bar to survey the gambling layouts across the packed room, he had given way to a hunch. From the tight roll of paper money in his pocket, he had peeled off two $10 bills and returned them to his pocket. Then, taking the rest, $200, he crossed the room to the cashier's stand and bought two blue poker chips, five reds and ten whites, all marked with the number 3. "The table next to the dance floor," the banker told him as he stared down unbelievingly at the neat stack of chips in his hand. Poker, like everything else in this town, was obviously for high stakes.

Those seventeen poker chips had represented all his worldly possessions, not taking into account his roan and saddle and the $20 in his pocket that would see him back to a friendly bunkhouse. He paid $15 for the deal and to draw two cards, the first hand at Table Three. Feeling three tens was not good enough to win, he sat back and watched the hand played out. He saw a $230 pot raked in by a man with two pair. That had been enough. The next hand it cost him a white and a red chip to take a wild chance on filling in a flush, and all but $10 of his money, his last two white chips, to hang along and call the bet. He had won $530 in laying down that flush. Then, in quick succession, he won on a full house, three queens, another flush, and finally the biggest hand of all, four sixes. His luck was phenomenal, surprising him even more than it did the others. They ran the betting sky-high and still couldn't stop him.

The house man across the table was looking uncomfortable and the inscrutable set to his face vanished gradually before a deep scowl. At the end of the seventh hand he pushed up his green eye shade and said tonelessly—"Game's closed for a few minutes, gentlemen."—and got up out of his chair to lose himself in the crowd over by the bar.

Dave Sanders looked down at the high stacks of blues, reds, and whites at his elbow. It was hard to believe. Over $6,000 here, and for three years now he'd been trying to scrape together a mere $1,000 as down payment for that six-section spread he wanted so badly at the foot of the Mogollons.

"I could stand some of that luck, stranger," sighed the player alongside as he bleakly eyed the table's empty green felt before him. "You cleaned me." He shrugged, pushed up out of his chair, and turned to leave.

Dave Sanders reached out and took a hold on his coat. "Here," he said, taking up a handful of blues and reds, "try that at another layout, mister. Your luck may change." Waving aside the man's astonished and profuse thanks, he scooped the remaining chips into his Stetson, cashed in at the banker's stand, and asked for $500 in counters for one of the faro layouts.

He thought the banker a little reluctant to count out the new set of chips, couldn't guess the reason. But as he walked up to the faro layout and put four blues on a square at the start of a deal, the dealer announced curtly: "Game's closed for an hour, gentlemen." He began to understand. He glanced toward Table Three; the game there had started again.

He sauntered over to Table Three with the deliberate conviction that he was headed into trouble. He took the one empty chair and waited for the hand to be finished. Then when the house man said quietly—"Game's closed for the night, gents."—he knew a thing for sure. They were closing the games on him.

"They told me this was a grown-up town," he drawled as the house man stood up. "They were wrong."

A sallow-faced man with two holstered six-guns slung low at this thighs beneath his long serge coat stood behind the chair of the player next to Dave Sanders. He said flatly: "Better clear out, stranger."

Dave looked up at him with a faint smile upturning the corners of his mouth. His eyes lost their glint of amusement. "Any good reason why I should?"

"Because I say so." This was Ned Olney, drawing $150 a week as one of the Nugget's three trouble-shooters.

Dave Sanders let out his breath in a long, gusty sigh. He shrugged his wide shoulders as he eased up out of his chair. The impassive set to his face didn't betray the settling anger that was running through him. He started to edge around Olney. All at once his right hand brushed up along his thigh in an easy, almost effortless move. The Colt .44 swiveled up out of his holster and settled into Olney's ribs.

"Take me to the boss," Dave drawled.

Olney's sallow face paled a shade. His deep gray eyes smeared over in a sultry killing light. "You won't get across that floor alive," he said.

"Then that means you won't, either."

Olney tried to read into this tall cowpuncher's even drawl some sign of nervousness or fear. It wasn't there. He saw Baird and Tolley and Stoop Gleeson, all Mike's men, edging through the crowd toward the table. He shook his head in a positive way that made them stop where they were and keep their distance. Then, feeling the blunt snout of the Colt pressing into his back, he started across the dance floor.

A few of the percentage girls had seen what was happening and moved out of the way with their partners. More than a few hadn't, and Olney was wishing that among the men still on the floor he'd find one friend who would have the guts to step in behind this stranger and pin his arms or beat him over the head with a six-gun—anything to give him the half second chance he needed. But on the forty-foot walk across to the office door, the weight of the weapon on his spine didn't once relax.

Olney opened the office door, stepped in, and heard the door close behind him. Kit Wales, the girl in the leather chair, saw who it was and gave an almost inaudible gasp of alarm. Mike was kneeling before the opened safe to one side of the desk, his back to the door. He growled: "What is it?"

"I'm here to find out why your gamblers shy from a man workin' off a winning streak," Dave Sanders said, his tone even in its drawl.

Ned Olney started to put in—"Boss, I did the best I . . ."—only abruptly to check his words at the expression on Mike's face as he turned from the safe.

"Dave!" Mike breathed hoarsely, unbelievingly. "Dave Sanders!"

The six-gun sagged in Dave's hand. "Mike!" he said, and stepped from behind the house man.

But before he had a chance to speak further, Mike Sanders, his brother, was holding up a hand to beckon him to silence. Mike nodded meaningly to the girl. "Kit, they're waitin' for you to sing out there. Ned, you go with her. I haven't seen this man in ten years."

Kit Wales, her glance fixed speculatively on this tall stranger, rose from her chair and came to the door. Dave's one look at her brought a touch of interest to his eyes, then a mute question, for he was asking himself how she came to be here and in these surroundings.

When the door had swung shut, Mike stepped over to the stove and threw in a round of wood. Then he said—"Have a seat, Dave."—and took the swivel chair at the desk. There was no attempt at a further greeting, and he gave no sign that this young brother was anything but a casual acquaintance. Dave took the leather chair as Mike queried: "What happened out there?"

"I was winning and they closed the games on me." Dave's smile had disappeared. His anger was gone now. He sat looking across at his older brother. Ten years had brought a change in Mike, one Dave couldn't quite grasp and wouldn't have believed had he been able to recognize it. But he did know Mike wasn't glad to see him and that hurt a little.

Mike said: "When a man with any sense starts losin' money at one of my layouts, he quits and goes home. When my gamblers start losin' to a man on a winnin' streak, they quit. It works both ways. Never buck a run of luck." He spent a moment lighting his cigar, getting the ash to burn evenly. "How come you found me?"

"I hit town tonight with a little over two

hundred dollars in my pocket. It started partin' company with me a little too fast and I thought I'd try and win some back. I came here, but I didn't know you were within five hundred miles. I didn't even know you were alive."

"Do they still have that reward out for me, kid?" Mike asked.

Dave reluctantly nodded. "'Most everyone's forgotten about it. Me and a few others figured that Maxwell pulled his gun first, that you gave him an even break. Why don't you go back and face that charge, Mike?"

Mike Sanders let a mirthless smile take possession of his face. "The sheriff was Maxwell's friend, wasn't he?" He shook his head. "I've been livin' as Mike Daniels too long. I couldn't go home a stray now."

Dave reached into his pocket and pulled out a roll of bills the size of his fist, the money the banker had given him a few minutes ago. "This is what I won, all but two hundred." He started to toss it across onto the desk.

"Keep it, kid." Mike puffed deliberately at his cigar and eyed Dave soberly through the bluish cloud of tobacco smoke. He envied this young brother, now grown to a man, for many things— the clean look about him, the level regard of an honest pair of eyes, the litheness of a tough, high-built frame.

As Dave returned the money to his pocket, he

was feeling a little uneasy before Mike's pointed stare. "This'll be enough to get me started on a place of my own, Mike. Thanks."

"Don't thank me. You won it." Mike shifted a little deeper into his swivel chair. "What kind of an outfit you goin' to buy, kid?"

"Six sections, a good house and barn."

Mike smiled thinly. "Why start a ten-cow outfit? Why not a real one?"

Dave felt a faint anger and uneasiness. "I don't get it, Mike."

"Stay here. Invest your money. Double it, triple it in half a year's time."

"How?'

Mike shrugged off-handedly. "Buy a lot and put up a livery barn for the mine teams. Start a restaurant. Hell, anything!" A sudden idea made him hesitate a moment. "Or even a hotel. How would you like to buy a hotel, kid?"

"How would I know how to run one?"

"Let someone else run it. That's what I do with this place." Mike took a deep drag on his cigar, coughed as the smoke bit his lungs. "Gus Mowry told me today he wants to get rid of the Mountain View."

"That's where I'm stoppin'. It isn't much of a place."

"Enough of a place so that Gus has made twenty thousand in the last year. But he struck pay dirt on a claim in the diggin's two days ago. Wants to get rid of the hotel. Say the word and it's yours for five thousand."

The unexpected had come so swiftly tonight that Dave Sanders wasn't at all certain his eyes and ears weren't deceiving him. Twenty minutes' play had put over $6,000 into his pocket. He'd met a brother he had worshipped as a boy of fourteen, ten years ago. Now Mike was giving him a chance to make more money, perhaps enough to buy that bigger twelve-section ranch in that grassy valley at the foot of the Iron Claws. Dave Sanders had once dreamed of owning that outfit and had never quite forgotten it.

Mike decided for him. The Nugget owner took a gold watch from his vest pocket, saw what time it was. "You've got about enough time to catch Gus before he turns in," he told Dave. "Offer him five thousand for the hotel, not a nickel more. He's been carryin' the deed in his pocket for two days and he'll sign tonight for cash. But don't tell him you know me." He got up out of the swivel chair and crossed to the door, put his hand on the knob.

"What's this Mowry got against you, Mike?" Dave was puzzled by his brother's request as he went to the door.

"Nothing. Only I've spent ten years buryin' a back trail, and I don't want people to get curious and start askin' you questions about me. And remember, I'm Mike Daniels, not Mike Sanders. See you tomorrow."

Mike Sanders, alias Mike Daniels, stood in the door to his office watching his young brother saunter off through the crowd gathered at the near end of the bar. The room was quiet. Kit Wales was singing. The girl stood on a raised platform at the near end of the bar, finishing the last few measures of an old favorite. Her voice, clear and carrying nicely through this barn-like room, added an unbelievable element of strangeness to a scene in which miners, gamblers, percentage girls, and camp followers stood, motionless and attentive; they had for the moment forgotten their impulses of wild recklessness and greed that made Aspen Gulch a wide-open, hard-bitten town. They showed Kit Wales a respect rarely shown a woman in this camp. And Mike Daniels for the hundredth time in these past few weeks realized what a find he had made in the girl.

The song ended abruptly amid a roar of applause. Ned Olney pushed his way through the crowd and back to the office door, clearing a lane for Kit who followed closely behind. She was smiling, beautiful, as she came into the office with Olney. But once the door was closed, her smile faded and Mike could see that it had been forced.

"What happened to your friend?" she asked him.

"The kid left about a minute ago."

"The kid?" she echoed. "I thought you called him Dave."

"Dave Sanders. He was a kid in knee pants when I last knew him," Mike told her. "I was . . . well, something like a big brother to him."

"You let him take the money?"

Mike nodded. He looked across at Olney with a wry smile coming to his face. "We've got Gus Mowry where we want him, Ned. That stranger's right now on his way to buy the hotel from Mowry with the money he won from me. Nice, eh?"

Olney said: "Gus told me this afternoon he'd sell out to anyone but you for five thousand . . . to you for a hundred thousand."

Mike laughed. "Gus takes a long time to forget."

"I've known for some time that Gus Mowry doesn't like you, Mike," the girl said. "Why is it?"

"Something about that stage that disappeared on its way out across the desert three weeks ago," Mike said offhandedly. "Gus had some money in the boot and lost it. He's got it in his craw my men did it."

"And did they?"

Mike eyed her levelly. "Is that any sort of a question to be asking me, Kit?"

The girl's face flushed. "I'm sorry, Mike," she said.

They were both thinking of the same thing, of how much she owed him. Four months ago, when the diggings had first opened up, Kit's father had brought her up here with him on a slender hope that he could be among the first to stake out a claim. She had stayed with a family in one of the three cabins that then made up the town while her father went on into the hills to prospect. There had been a solid week of cold rain and sleet, and one day two men had packed her father's body down out of the hills wrapped in a dirty tarpaulin. He had died of pneumonia. Mike had found her shortly afterward; he had heard that she was penniless and that she could sing. He gave her a job, decent enough, of singing three times each day to the crowds that swarmed into his new saloon. Now she had money, a nice room at the hotel, and the respect and admiration of every man in the camp.

"This opens things up, Ned," Mike now said. "I'll get the kid to let us put a bar in the room off the lobby. There's another room in back. We'll put Charley Mott in there with an assay outfit." He shot the house man a significant glance.

Ned Olney nodded, smiled broadly. "Things are lookin' up. You ought to take out a thousand a week."

Kit Wales had many times been in here when Mike talked to Olney or one of his other men in this vague manner of understatement. She had liked Mike Daniels from the first, for he had been kind and thoughtful and she saw in him a natural leader of men. Yet at times like this an undercurrent of restlessness and fear took its hold on her; once or twice she had suspected Mike of not being quite honest but had immediately put the thought from her mind as disloyal.

She didn't want to think about this again. She said: "Mike, I'm tired. Could Ned take me to the hotel?"

Mike looked at her sharply, concern in his glance. "Why don't you take the day off tomorrow, Kit? Ned'll bring the chestnut around in the mornin' and you can ride out into the hills and breathe some of this stale air out of your lungs."

"Thank you, Mike. I think I will."

He went with her to the door and told her as she went out: "Give me a minute with Ned before you go." He closed the door, turned to his house man. "Better start the word goin' the rounds that we're in the market for high-grade, Ned. We ought to have that alley room at the hotel for Charley by tomorrow night."

"You sure this Sanders will come in on a deal like this, boss?"

Mike laughed. "The kid'll do what I tell him. He won't know a damned thing about it."

"How much of this high-grade can Charley Mott take care of? We don't want every man in the diggin's to know about it. This sheriff is thick in the head but he's got a pair of eyes."

Mike frowned thoughtfully. "Get twenty good men. And tell 'em we're buying nothing but the finest picture rock they can lay hands on. There's no use runnin' this business unless we all make real money."

Ned Olney grinned. "They won't mind that," he said as he went out.

II

Dave Sanders had to admit that Mike had ideas for making money. The morning after Gus Mowry had signed over the deed to the Mountain View, it took Mike two hours to carry his argument for installing a bar in the room off the lobby. "If you're here to make money, make all you can as soon as you can," he insisted. "We'll put in the bar and split fifty-fifty. In six months you'll be a rich man, kid, rich enough to buy an outfit big enough to take ten men to work it."

"But all I want is a place to run a few critters to work by myself," was Dave's answer.

"Kid, a man spends nine-tenths of his life strainin' his guts to earn enough to feed his mouth. I want to see you do better than that."

A reawakening of the respect and awe Dave had felt for this older brother in boyhood was what finally made him give in, that and the fact that Mike seemed more human and friendly than last night. So at two that afternoon the carpenters started work. At eight that night the bar was open, doing business with two barkeeps having all they could do to fill the orders of a crowd that packed the small room and fought for chairs at the two poker layouts. The second night Mike had to send over another barkeep to help the others take care of the business, and the money rattled into the cash drawer.

It was two days before Dave met Charley Mott, who brought along a note from Mike. Mott was old, grizzled, and walked with a bad limp, and the note he handed Dave read:

This man is broke and having a bad run of luck. He got his bad leg in a mine explosion at Deadwood. He may be able to make a living running an assay office in that room behind the bar, the one we fixed up as a storeroom. Let him alone and we'll see how it works out.

Mike

Mott was quiet, gruff of manner, and moved a bed and a few belongings into the room behind the bar. Dave was proud to think that Mike was helping a man down and out. He didn't see much of Mott and in a week's time noticed only three customers going back to the assay office behind the end poker tables.

Gus Mowry's clerk stayed on and took care of most of the business at the desk. He didn't particularly like the idea of Dave's lowering the charge for a cot from $5 to $3 dollars, nor of

Dave's spending $130 for twenty-seven cots in the two bunkrooms along the hallway behind the lobby. When Dave brought in two men to clean out the place and told the Chinese laundryman to call for a change of blankets to be washed twice a week, the clerk said: "Hell, these geezers won't feel right sleepin' in clean beds, Sanders. That's money thrown down the drain."

"You're handin' me anywhere between a hundred and twenty and a hundred and fifty dollars a day out of the cash drawer," Dave told him. "Those cots work three eight-hour shifts a day for me, and, if I can't afford to give clean blankets twice a week, I ought to quit business."

The clerk shook his head but after that kept his opinions to himself.

On the fifth morning Kit Wales came from her room at the end of the hall and found Dave at the desk in the lobby. She laid five gold double eagles on the counter before him. "Time to pay my rent."

This girl was Mike's friend and, therefore, his; he had accepted her as such. He had seen her three times since that first night, twice in Mike's office and once on the street. He had heard her sing once and hadn't been able to forget her voice. His curiosity at finding her working in a saloon had made him inquire and get the story of her father's death. And now each time he saw her he was impressed with her freshness and her smile as contrasted to the tawdry cheapness of the

71

women on the street and in the saloons. He liked it that she called him—"Dave"—instead of—"kid"—as Mike did.

"But that cracker box of a room isn't worth a hundred a month," he protested as she pushed the money across. "It isn't worth half that."

"I can't get another in town for any less, Dave," she said, smiling up at him. "I know what you're thinking. But this is a boom town. The sooner you get onto things and forget your conscience, the better off you'll be." A sound from the back of the lobby took her attention and she turned to look into the saloon room to see the boards of the floor torn away and a pile of dirt and rock rubble heaped against one wall. She asked: "What's going on in there?"

"Mike's men need more room. Charley Mott and his assay outfit in that back room don't leave them enough space for storage. They're diggin' a cellar." Dave shook his head and the expression on his lean face was one of outright bewilderment. "I'll never understand it. Every morning I bank enough money from this hotel and the saloon to keep me in grub for half a year. The most I ever corralled in one month before this was fifty-five dollars."

"I thought Mike told me you had your eye on a ranch down by the Mogollons."

"Sure, but . . ."

"Dave, the money you're making here isn't even

72

small change to what some of the claim owners are taking out. The lowest pay for pick and shovel work in the mines up the gulch is twelve dollars a day. The swamper in the Nugget gets ten and makes another ten every day panning gold dust from the sawdust under the banker's stand. Take all that comes your way and remember that it's probably the only time in your life you'll ever be able to lay your hands on easy money."

Her voice was edged with a certain bitterness that Dave couldn't understand. She explained it a moment later. "My father was poor, always hoping for the day when he'd be able to give me things. He died trying for that day. You should be thankful you'll never have to go through a thing like that."

On the way down the plank walk toward the Nugget a few minutes later, Kit Wales was wondering why she was siding with Mike in keeping Dave Sanders here in Aspen Gulch. She knew instinctively that there was something underhanded in Mike's having advised Dave to buy the hotel and in the opening of the bar and the assay office, and here she was helping Mike's plan along by urging Dave to stay when the thing she knew he wanted more than anything else was to be miles away, alone in the saddle with his thoughts shaping a less bewildering pattern.

All at once she did know why she sided with Mike. It was because each day she looked forward to seeing Dave and talking with him, because even the thought of him brought up in her a strange excitement, an interest she had never before felt in a man. The realization left her for a moment stunned, but then a deep happiness grew strong within her and she hurried on along the walk. She wanted to tell Mike about this.

The Nugget's bar was drawing customers even this early in the morning. A few of the men spoke and tipped their hats to her respectfully as she went back along the room. She saw Ned Olney and a workman with grimy face and hands cross the dance floor ahead of her and go into Mike's office. She hesitated to go in, knowing that Mike would probably have business with his house man. So she went to the piano, which stood close to the office door, and sat down and started looking through some new sheet music that had come in on yesterday afternoon's stage.

She heard the faint *squeak* of hinges and looked toward the office door, thinking that Ned and the workman were on their way out. But the latch had failed to catch and the door stood ajar two inches, then, as she looked back at her music, she heard Mike's booming voice say hoarsely: "Bill, are you crazy? This couldn't have come out of that hole!"

"It did, Mike," came a strange voice Kit knew must be the workman's. "From right below the bar in that back room behind the lobby."

There was a moment's silence. Then Mike's voice rasped: "Who else knows about it?"

"No one but me."

"Can you keep your mouth shut for a week . . . for, say, a thousand dollars, Bill?"

"Sure, boss."

"Then get back there and fill up that hole. Board up the floor and pull your men off the job. Tell Sanders we've decided it's costin' too much, that we'll get along without it. Tell him anything you want, so long as he doesn't get wise."

Kit moved away from the piano barely in time to keep from being seen as the door opened and Ned and the workman came out. She was standing at the empty lunch counter asking the apron for a glass of water, when Ned Olney walked past. He saw her, hesitated, then came up to her and said: "Mike wants to see you, Kit."

He went along with her to the office but remained at the door only long enough to wink in at Mike and say: "You wanted to see Kit about Sanders, didn't you, boss?"

As the door closed behind Olney and she faced Mike alone, Kit Wales was trying to keep the stark fear that was in her from showing on her face. She hadn't quite grasped the whole truth of what she had heard—that something had been discovered in the Mountain View's new cellar, something Mike wanted badly enough to pay a common workman $1,000 not to tell Dave about it.

When she dared a glance at Mike, who sat in the swivel chair behind his desk, she was seeing a new man. Perhaps the change was in her rather than in him, but in that moment he looked older, not handsome as she had always thought him, and in his eyes was a brightness of cold calculation and greed she could now read rightly. She hated him.

"Kit, we've been looking for the kid. Know where we can find him?"

"He was at the hotel a minute ago." Her voice sounded unnatural, but if Mike noticed, he gave no indication of it. He was too absorbed by some inner thought.

"I'd like to see him right away. Would you mind going back and getting him?"

"Is . . . is something wrong?" she asked in a small voice, wishing as soon as the words were out that she hadn't spoken.

But once again some inner abstraction made him blind to her nervousness. He laughed sharply, shook his head. "Far from it. Dave told me yesterday he was sick of the place, wanted to leave. So I started lookin' around for a buyer for the hotel. I think I've found one. I want to see what sort of an offer he'll take. Tell him to hurry, will you?"

She nodded and was glad to be out of the room, away from him and alone with her tormented thoughts. The two minutes it took her to walk back to the Mountain View she spent wondering what she would tell Dave, fighting down her feeling of gratitude and obligation toward Mike for the way he had treated her since her father's death.

When she stood at the lobby counter, facing Dave, she was still uncertain of herself. That uncertainty must have shown on her face, for as he looked at her Dave's eyes mirrored surprise and concern.

She told him: "Mike wants to see you, right away."

"Something's happened, Kit. What is it?"

"Mike says he's found a buyer for the hotel."

His frown faded and its place was taken by a wide smile. He came from behind the counter, saying: "That's the best news I've had since I hit this town." He took down his Stetson from the hat rack at the end of the counter and started for the door.

"Dave!" she called, and he stopped and turned to face her. "Dave . . . I . . . I can't tell you why I'm asking this, but I want you to promise me you won't sell the Mountain View." She realized that her face had taken on a flush of embarrassment, that her words sounded weak, uncertain.

His expression was one of puzzlement. "But this is what I've been waitin' for, Kit. I want to get out of this town, clear of this country. I don't like it. I . . ."

"Would it make any difference if I told you that I want you to stay, that you'd be doing it for me?"

This was the only thing that occurred to her, the only appeal she could make without betraying Mike's confidence, the confidence she owed him. Then, when she saw the look of confusion that came to Dave's face, she added hurriedly: "I can't tell you any more, Dave. But you must trust me. And you mustn't tell Mike we've talked about it. Only please tell him you won't sell."

"That's all, Kit?" he queried tonelessly, gone abruptly sober.

"That's all." A foreboding of failure lay deeply within her as she turned from him and went back along the hallway to her room.

That picture of her stayed with him on his way to the Nugget. He could still see the proud tilt of her head, the depth of emotion that had been mirrored in her green eyes. He wondered what lay behind her strange, unexplained request, then, as he opened the door to Mike's office, he put it all into the back of his mind.

"Take the easy chair, kid," Mike said, indicating the leather chair. He pushed a box of cigars across the desk. "Smoke?"

Dave shook his head, recognizing in Mike's forgetful gesture a sign of nervousness, for Mike had on another occasion offered his brother a cigar only to have Dave tell him that he never smoked them.

"Kid, I think I'm onto something. I think I've found you a buyer for the Mountain View."

Dave's hands were busy sifting tobacco from a Durham sack onto a wheat-straw cigarette paper. Without looking up at Mike, he gave a laugh: "I meant to stop in yesterday and tell you to forget that, Mike. I've decided to hang here a bit longer. Might even buy up one of these small claims and develop it." He licked the paper, put the cigarette in his mouth, and only then looked up blandly at Mike.

His glance was in time to catch a strained, hard expression on his brother's face. Mike was tense, his eyes narrowed in an almost hateful look in that brief split second before his narrow face once more assumed its cloak of affability. "Never thought I'd hear you talk like that, kid. Maybe you'll forget it when I tell you this man's offering twelve thousand for the Mountain View. He's a tenderfoot from back East, a sucker, bound he's goin' to buy a business and clean up a pile of money."

"That's my idea, Mike. I'd be off my head to sell when everything's comin' my way."

Mike leaned across with elbows on the desk top. "We might make him boost the offer to fifteen thousand. If you want to stay, take the money and I'll buy you the sweetest small claims in the diggin's. Up at the head of the gulch. They haven't started workin' that yet, but there's a fortune up there for the man willing to go after it."

Schmaling Mem. Pub. Library
501 Tenth Avenue
Fulton, IL 61252

Dave smiled, shook his head. "Thanks, Mike, but I'm stayin'. The hotel isn't for sale."

Mike's manner had gradually lost its friendliness. He was intent, persuasive. He had the look now of a shrewd and calculating man; there was something Dave defined as greed in his glance, too, although he couldn't explain why it should be there.

"Kid, I've treated you right since you came here," Mike said flatly. "I've put you in the way of making some money, big money. My advice now is to cash in and clear out. You aren't the sort for this kind of life. Hell, you think I want to see you wind up like me, driftin', livin' hard, knowing nobody but these saloon tramps? Get out of it, cut it off clean, and live like you were meant to."

"Mike, you're spooked over something that isn't goin' to happen," Dave said, getting up out of the chair. "I'll stick around a while longer. I'll have my look at this wild town, and, when I'm ready, I'll pull out. Not before."

There was a quality of stoniness to his brother's voice that carried its warning to Mike. He shrugged his heavy shoulders, waved a hand in a careless gesture that came too late to deceive Dave. "Have it your own way. Only you've heard my side of this, kid, and, if anything goes wrong, don't blame me."

"I'll watch that end of it," Dave said as he went to the door.

"By the way," Mike said. "That crew diggin' the basement has run into some hard goin'. We've decided to shovel back that muck we've dug out and go on usin' the back room." He opened a drawer of his desk, took out some papers, and started sorting through them, making it obvious that the interview was over.

Dave left.

At the Mountain View he passed the lobby desk and went back along the hallway to the door of Kit Wales's room. He knocked, and in a moment heard her light step inside.

She gave a visible start at sight of him. He noticed that particularly. "Kit, Mike offered me fifteen thousand for the hotel. I turned him down."

"Thank you for trusting me, Dave," she said, low-voiced.

"Is that all you have to say about it?"

"That's all I can say, Dave."

He left her and turned and went back along the hallway a decidedly puzzled man. The offer on the hotel had been ridiculously high. The promise Kit Wales had exacted of him was something else ridiculous and without any explanation. The look she had given him, one of gratitude and tenderness, was another thing that was hard to believe.

Coming into the lobby, the sound of dirt slurring along the boards of the saloon room floor made him turn that way. The four workmen were shoveling the mound of dirt and rock back into the hole dug directly beneath the floor joists. Dave remembered Mike's mention of the trouble the men were having sinking the hole. He walked to the edge of the torn-up floor and looked down. Something immediately struck him as being peculiar. Only a foot of the hole's depth had been filled in. At the bottom the rock showed rotten and crumbling and mixed with dirt along the firm sides of the walls. He looked for a pick mark, couldn't see one below the three-foot level. And the hole was already nearly six feet deep, almost finished. The last three feet had been nothing but shovel work. Yet Mike had claimed that his men had struck hard going!

III

One of the workmen, a heavy-framed man in bib overalls, sauntered over to Dave. "The boss decided to fill it in," he announced. "Guess he thinks there's all the room they need in back."

Dave nodded casually, trying to appear disinterested as he crossed the lobby to his desk. Here was something as puzzling as Mike's strange offer to buy the hotel, as puzzling as Kit Wales's even stranger insistence that he should turn down Mike's offer.

During the next hour he waited with a stubborn

patience. He was finally rewarded in seeing three of the workmen come out of the closed room and leave. He heard one man in there, hammering the floor back into place, and decided that now was the time he'd been waiting for. As he crossed the lobby to the closed doors, Kit Wales came out of the back hallway and went out the door onto the street, not seeing him.

He opened one of the double doors to the saloon room, went in. The carpenter was on his knees on the floor and looked back at him over his shoulder once and went back to work. No one else was in the room.

"Charley Mott in?" Dave asked him.

The carpenter gave him a puzzled look. "No one here by that name. You'll have to ask one of the others," he said. "I was only hired this mornin'."

Satisfied that this wasn't one of Mike's men, Dave went on back past the poker tables and to the door of the assay office. He tried the knob; the door was locked. He knocked, and in a few seconds the lock grated and the door swung open. Charley Mott, in his trousers and minus his shirt and socks and with his hair mussed, blinked up at him. He had obviously been asleep; the room beyond was dark behind drawn shades.

"You're sleepin' late, Charley," Dave said as he pushed on into the room, making the oldster move unwillingly aside.

"Had a heavy night," Mott muttered. "What can I do for you, Sanders?"

"Show me your layout here. I'd like to know a little more about this assaying business."

Suspicion flared alive in Mott's eyes and was gone an instant later. "Help yourself," he said nervously, closing the door.

Dave stepped to the window at the back of the room, ran up the shade, and looked out onto the alley. A door into the alley stood in the rear wall four feet away. Facing the room once more, Dave noted its sparse furnishings. Charley's cot was along the right wall and directly ahead of an eight-foot-long counter. On the counter were two sets of balance scales, one large and one small. Several sacks of what Dave judged were ore samples lay on the floor behind the counter and under a heavy slab table on which stood an assortment of crucibles and retorts, a small ore crusher, and four bulging glass carboys of acid. Beyond the table squatted a small portable charcoal furnace. Next to that was a rectangular safe.

"Looks like you're havin' good business," Dave commented.

"So-so. Them samples are mostly my own. I do a little prospectin' on the side."

Mott's answer sounded reasonable enough. There was nothing here to rouse Dave's suspicions. At the front of the room, directly behind the bar on the opposite side of the wall, the carpenters had nailed up a head-high partition. Cases of whiskey, a few boxes of assorted sizes of glasses, and three barrels of beer were stored behind it.

Dave started for the door leading back to the saloon room. As he put his hand on the knob, a heavy pounding sounded from the room's alley door. The oldster gave a start and seemed to go tense at the sound.

"Go ahead and answer it, Charley," Dave said. "I'll wait."

Charley Mott shot him a wary glance, and then limped barefooted to the rear door. He opened it a bare two inches, so that Dave couldn't see who stood in the alley.

Charley held a muttered conversation with someone outside. Dave heard him say: "You're drunk, Simmons. Go home." Then all at once a man's thick voice out there rose in anger. "Damned if I'll come back later! Take it now. And get this straight, Mott! You shorted me on the last pay-off. Don't try it again. This stuff was hard enough to steal without your robbin' me!"

Mott, plainly desperate, reached out the door and brought his hand in again holding the wire handle of a two-quart dinner pail. He slammed the door shut, set the dinner pail on the floor, and turned to Dave.

He opened his mouth to speak, shut it again at what he saw. Dave was coming toward him across the room. He shot a desperate glance at his cot where his holstered six-gun hung from a nail on the wall.

"Hand it over, Charley," Dave said, indicating the dinner pail. "I'd like a look."

The oldster picked up the pail, held it out. But as Dave reached for it, he dropped the pail and his hand snatched at Dave's holstered six-gun. Dave wheeled out of the way, doubled his fist, and chopped in a blow that took Mott on the point of the jaw. The oldster fell heavily, rolled onto his back, and lay still.

The dinner pail was brimming with crushed rock, some of it grayish in color, but many pieces the color of rust and flecked with bright yellow spots. Dave took out his clasp knife and gouged out one of the large yellow crystals. Even his scant knowledge was enough to tell him that this was gold.

In the next two minutes his thoughts left him dazed, unbelieving. He had heard of high-grading, knew what the words meant. As the realization came to him that Mike was crooked, dishonest to the core, he felt nothing but pity and shame for his brother. But then he looked beyond that dishonesty and saw how Mike had been using him; from deep inside him a spark of stubborn anger was fanned alive. Then, when he thought of Kit Wales, when he remembered the feeling of gratitude she must feel toward the man who had befriended her and what use Mike might make of that blind devotion, a coolness settled along his nerves, and he went out into the saloon room and through the lobby. He paused at the desk only long enough to sort through some papers in one of the drawers. What he finally found and put in his pocket before he went out onto the street was the deed to the Mountain View.

Mike had long ago realized that in Kit Wales he had the biggest drawing card in his business. He used her accordingly, scheduling her first appearance of the day shortly after eleven in the morning, attracting to the Nugget the lucrative noon-hour trade. He had found that a heavy demand on the free-lunch counter at the back of the bar meant a busy afternoon.

That morning he sent Ned Olney out to bring Kit to the office as soon as she had finished singing. He wasn't trusting himself to face her until they were alone. As the last trailing note of her third song died in a smother of applause beyond the office door, he took out a cigar and lit it. He went to the stove and threw in a chunk of wood although the room was warm enough. It was as plain a gesture of nervousness as the quick shifting of his heavy wide shoulders.

Olney opened the door a moment later, let Kit Wales step into the room past him, and discreetly closed it again.

"You wanted to see me?" the girl asked.

Mike smiled down at her and nodded, pulling the leather chair a little closer to the desk before she sat in it. He tilted back in his swivel chair and for the moment was unable to speak what was on his mind. He was too absorbed by his thoughts to notice her manner, which matched his own nervousness.

"Kit," he said finally, "I've decided we ought to clear out of this town."

"We?" she said, a faint surprise in her glance.

Mike nodded, went on hurriedly: "I've got a deal on now that ought to net me close to a half a million dollars. That's all a man needs, Kit. I want you to marry me."

As he paused, waiting for her answer, the *squeak* of door hinges sounded across the room's stillness. He whipped his glance that way to see Dave Sanders standing in the opening. He began gruffly—"Men aren't in the habit of coming in here . . ."—but broke off as Dave swung the door shut and leaned back against it.

"Go on, Mike," Dave drawled. "I want to hear Kit's answer."

His blue eyes had taken on the coldness of winter ice. Kit Wales saw Mike's face go purple at this calm insolence, but before he had the chance to speak, she said haltingly: "Dave, you . . . you shouldn't have come here."

Dave's bleak smile held. Reaching behind him, he turned the key in the lock, took it to the stove, lifted the lid, and dropped it onto the hot coals. Mike suddenly breathed a curse and lunged up out of his chair, rasping: "What the hell goes on here?"

As his brother moved, Dave took two steps that put him alongside the desk. For a moment they stood face to face, Mike lacking a bare inch of matching Dave's tallness but looking decidedly the heavier of the two. Abruptly Dave reached out a hand, drawled—"Sit down!"—and pushed Mike roughly by the shoulder so that he went off balance and sat down heavily in the chair. "Mike, I've just had a look at that set-up of Charley Mott's in the back room. Is that any way to treat your brother?"

Mike growled: "What Mott does is no business of mine. See here, kid, I'll . . ."

"Brother!" Kit cried. "You two are brothers?"

Dave nodded. "Weren't you onto that?"

The girl was staring at Mike with a loathing in her eyes. "You're Dave's brother and still you'd do a thing like that?" she breathed. Then a subtle change rode through her and her head came up and she said tonelessly: "And you asked me to marry you. Mike Daniels, I hate you."

"Mike Sanders, you mean," Dave drawled. His glance hadn't moved off the saloon owner. He reached to a back pocket of his Levi's and brought out the deed, tossing it onto the desk. "There it is, Mike, the thing you wanted so bad. It's yours.

Won't cost you a cent. I don't know why you wanted it and I don't know what's wrong here. But you've got what you wanted. I'm pullin' out."

"Mike's men found gold in that cellar this morning, Dave," Kit Wales put in.

"See here!" Mike blustered.

"That sounds like you, Mike," Dave intoned. "A brotherly act . . . robbery!" His smile now made a hard line of his mouth. He took off his Stetson and sailed it into the corner beyond the stove; it glanced off the stovepipe that went through the partition to turn in an elbow above the dance floor and go out through the roof beyond. Next he took off his vest and threw it after the Stetson, drawling: "The hotel and a gold mine underneath! All the high-grade that's stolen out of the diggin's! Mike, you'll be a rich man before you know it. Only before I leave, I'm goin' to take you apart and see which wheel is missin' from the works in your thick skull. Get onto your feet!"

Mike's look slowly changed. His face turned a beet-red, his thin lips curled down into a sneer. He pushed back a bare inch in his swivel chair, and, as he moved, his right hand edged in beneath the lapel of his coat toward the spring holster at his left armpit.

Dave drawled: "Go ahead. Make your try if you want it that way."

All at once Mike remembered Ned Olney's words that first night when Dave had been a stranger making a cleaning at Number Three poker layout. He looked at the holster along Dave's thigh and his hand came from under his coat.

Kit Wales said in a voice muted by fear: "Please, Dave, please . . ."

Mike lunged at that moment. He pushed the swivel chair to the back wall, put his whole weight behind his arms, and pushed the desk over. As it fell with a crash of splitting wood, its edge caught Dave on the shins, knocked him off balance. He fell, rolled clear and onto his feet again. He came around the desk and met Mike's head-down rush with two stiff uppercuts that rocked the saloon owner back onto his heels.

Mike covered his face and stepped back out of range. For one split second he looked at his brother, sizing him up. It was as though he wondered how this tall, flat-framed man twenty pounds lighter than he could pack so much power into his fists. Blood streamed from his nose and from a gash over his left eye.

Dave said—"Come on, Mike! I'm likin' this!"—and took one step toward him.

Mike knew one brand of fighting and it had served him through half a hundred saloon brawls. He reached out and in a lightning move snatched the swivel chair from the floor. It rose in a high arc toward Dave's head. There was only one way to dodge it. Dave fell backward onto the down-slanting desk top. The chair grazed his left shoulder and sailed on past to smash squarely into the stove and tip it over.

The stove pipe fell to the floor with a crash and in a smother of ash dust and flying sparks as Kit Wales screamed and ran to the door. Outside the thin partition came the sound of the stove pipe crashing to the dance floor. Someone shouted beyond the door.

Dave lay helplessly on his back watching Mike's hand streak in under his coat. The saloon owner's fist came out holding a stubby pearl-handled Colt .38. Dave kicked out with his right foot. His boot caught Mike on the wrist; the gun exploded upward toward the ceiling as it flew from his hand. A split second later he threw himself on Dave.

There was barely time for Dave to raise his knees to his chest. Mike's weight against his knees drove the breath out of his lungs. Then, pushing with all his strength as Mike's fists drove in at his face, he threw Mike off and rolled onto the floor. Mike hit the wall hard, kicked wildly at Dave's face as he rolled over. Dave reached up and caught his brother's left boot and twisted. Mike staggered off balance, and backed away to give Dave barely the time to come to his feet.

They stood toe to toe, swinging wildly, each putting all the weight of his body behind his driving fists. Behind them someone shouted hoarsely beyond the door. A gun thundered its hollow blast. The lock shattered and flew off the door and Dave drove in a smashing blow that mashed Mike's nose to his face and made his knees buckle. As the saloon owner dropped to hands and knees, the door crashed back against the wall and Dave wheeled in time to see Ned Olney standing beyond with his hands lifting his two guns from holsters. At the same time he saw that the carpet over by the stove was in flames, that smoke was rolling toward the ceiling.

Dave crouched, and his right hand blurred down and up in a move too fast for eye to follow. Kit Wales was standing dangerously close to the door as Dave's gun fell into line. He slipped his thumb from the hammer almost too quickly in his haste to beat Olney's draw. Yet as the house man's guns exploded powder flame, the man's body jerked backward convulsively. Dave felt a blow take him on the outside of his right thigh. The cloth of his left shirt sleeve ripped as the other slug cut through it.

Olney was down on his knees, a smear of blood showing along his white shirt front and a red froth flecking his pale lips. Then, as he made one last effort to swing his guns into line, Dave emptied his Colt in a staccato thunder that drove the house man sprawling onto his back.

Suddenly he saw that Kit was no longer in sight. He turned, and, as he moved, an explosion beat across the stillness from behind him. He wheeled that way in time to look across the smoke-filled room and see Mike's pearl-handled weapon fall from Kit Wales's hand. She was staring, horrified, at something along the back wall.

It was Mike. He sat with his back to the wall, eyes already fixed in the glazed stare of death. In his hand was clutched a double-barreled Derringer, the hammers cocked. Within his reach a drawer sagged open from the overturned desk. He had remembered that Derringer in the drawer, taken it out, and Kit Wales's shot had caught him in the back.

"The door, Dave!" Kit called in a voice touched with hysterical fear.

Dave lunged out of the way at the exact instant an exploding concussion beat the air. Plaster dust sifted down off the back wall. A man with a shotgun at his shoulder stood beyond Ned Olney's body on the dance floor. Dave whipped up his heavy .44 and threw it. The weapon caught the man fully in the face, made him scream in pain.

Then, choking as the acrid smoke of the burning carpet bit into his lungs, Dave knocked the door shut and dragged the heavy desk over against it. He moved out of the way barely in time as the panel was splintered by three bullets that slapped into the opposite wall.

"The window, Kit!" Dave called as he picked up

the broken swivel chair. He couldn't see the girl in the smoke-fogged room. But through the smoke he could see the dim blue of light that came through the high small window facing the passageway between the saloon and the adjoining building. He raised the chair and sent it whirling at the window.

The crash of splintering boards and falling glass sounded above the crackling of the flames that were now licking up along the thin inner partition. Kit was alongside him and Dave was lifting her toward the window. She caught a hold, pulled herself through. Dave followed a second later.

As he dropped into the littered passageway beside her, Kit cried: "Dave, you're hurt!"

There was a dark red smear along his right thigh, and, as he put his weight on the leg, a lance of pain stabbed him in the thick muscle.

He took her by the arm: "Head for the street."

His last look back along the passageway as they made the crowded walk showed him a thick plume of smoke billowing out of the open window. A crowd jammed the walk in front of the Nugget's swing doors and someone yelled: "Fire! Get the buckets!"

Dave took the girl's arm and led her away down the walk. "Get into your room," he told her as they came even with the entrance to the Mountain View.

She felt his hold relax on her arm. He started

ahead along the walk. She took two quick steps that put her even with him and asked: "Where are you going, Dave?"

"Livery barn."

"You're . . . you're leaving?" she asked in a voice that made him stop and look down at her.

"There isn't much else to do," he said.

"You're leaving me?" she asked incredulously. Something he saw in her eyes confused him. "I couldn't take you with me, Kit. There'll be a posse behind me all the way to the state line."

"But why do you go?" she asked. "You've done nothing wrong."

Dave smiled bleakly and nodded down the street. Smoke was pouring out the Nugget's swing doors now and thin wisps of smoke were curling out from beneath the building roof.

"You didn't do that, Dave. Mike did. The thing to do is go straight to the sheriff."

"He wouldn't believe me."

"He'd believe me. Mark Healy was one of my dad's friends. He knows I wouldn't lie." Kit Wales held out her hand and in it was the crumpled Mountain View deed. "And we'll need this, Dave."

He frowned as he looked down at the dog-eared grimy piece of paper. "I don't want it even if it is sittin' on a gold mine. All I want is to get out and ride clear of this place."

"That's all I want, too, Dave. But we'll need something to live on, won't we?"

He caught the inference to her words with a suddenness that left him weak. "We?" he echoed. "You mean . . . you . . . ?"

A smile came to her face, one with a tenderness that melted the last trace of bitterness out of Dave Sanders. There, in plain sight of half a hundred people running along the walk toward the Nugget, he took her in his arms.

Hell for Homesteaders

This story was completed in April, 1938 and submitted by Jon Glidden's agent to Street & Smith's *Western Story Magazine* on May 13, 1938. Editorial changes were requested and a revised version of the story was completed on July 1, 1938 and the story was accepted for publication on July 27, 1938. The author was paid $189 upon publication under this title in the issue dated November 5, 1938.

I

Bill English and Red Bone knew they'd been lucky. Ten days back, with half a winter's pay in their pockets, they'd ridden into Buffalo Springs and read the notice on the Land Office door. The Buffalo Springs Navajo Reservation was to be opened to homesteaders the next day.

They'd never heard of Buffalo Springs before that day, nor did they know what kind of land was being offered under the Homestead Act. But with a desire common to all cowpunchers—that of eventually owning their own brand—they had taken a look at the survey maps and ridden up Antelope Creek. They found and staked two sections of unbelievably fine graze, and the next day they filed on it, paying their $34 each, and not really believing in their good luck until their names were duly recorded in the county deed book. After that, they'd hired a wagon and a team and hauled a load of spooled barbed wire to the site where they intended to build their cabin.

It had taken them these ten days to cut cedar posts and string all that wire and make a start on the one-room cabin. This morning they had started at sunup for town, intending to buy enough wire to finish the fence and to return the wagon and team and buy one of their own.

Now, as the trail swung away from the rich grasslands of the creek bottom to bring them within sight of the distant town, Red Bone heaved a lusty sigh and said: "We just ain't this lucky, Bill. Hell, with all that free range to the west, we'll have one of the biggest outfits in the country in five years."

"And what's the joker in that?" Bill English had the same misgivings as his partner, but he wasn't going to admit them. The night before, unable to sleep, English had walked out to the line of their new fence and stumbled onto something that was his reason for wearing a holstered six-gun at his thigh this morning. He had seen three mounted riders following the line of their wire, and one of these, as he drew abreast of English in the darkness, had called to the man nearest him: "It ought to be easy enough to pull down!"

The fence was still standing in the morning. Bill hadn't told Red about it, but he wasn't so sure now that they were to have an easy time of it. Today in town, he intended asking a few questions about their neighbors.

"You and me have nursed critters for ten years at forty dollars a month and grub," Red said. "It ain't natural to just fall into something like this. It ain't natural, I tell . . ."

He left his thought unfinished and suddenly raised a hand and pointed. English, looking off to the left of the trail, saw something that immediately made him rein the team to a stand-still.

Twenty yards away, half hidden by a *chamiza* bush, lay a huddled shape they made out to be a man's. English swung down off the seat and ran over there, Red at his heels. For a moment they stood there looking down at the man, unable to believe what they saw.

Then Bill English knelt beside the doubled-up figure. "Easy, partner," he said. "We'll have you out of this in a hurry."

He wasn't sure until the eyes opened that the man was alive. Dried blood smeared the round face, there was a deep gash over one eye, and the strands of barb wire that bound the man in a jackknifed, cramped position had cut his wrists and arms and back until his blue denim was all but covered with brownish red stains. Bill and Red worked fast, and as gently as they could, and finally Red lifted the man to a sitting position and pulled the dirty rag gag from his mouth. A moment later English was back from the wagon with the canteen, uncorking it to give the stranger a long drink through swollen lips.

"Better?" Bill asked as he lowered the canteen.

The stranger seemed dazed, and a look of half fear edged his glance, but he managed to mumble: "I thought I was done for."

"Don't bother to talk now," English said. "Let's get you on your pins and over to the wagon. We're headed for town and can take you to a sawbones."

They'd driven half a mile farther, with the wounded stranger riding between them on the seat, before he spoke again. "I thought at first you was part of the bunch that left me there last night. Thought you'd come back to finish the job."

Bill English shook his head. "We're home-steadin' up the creek. This is Red, I'm Bill. You want to tell us about it?"

Instead of answering his question directly, the stranger breathed: "You're homesteadin' on Antelope, too?" He laughed harshly. "You'd better get ready to pull out. I work for Orndorff."

"Who's Orndorff?" Red Bone asked.

"My boss. His place is four miles above yours. He's been intendin' to get down to call on you, but hasn't had the time. He brought me and four others with him. We've taken out five sections. It seems like the lot of us ought to have saved ourselves the trouble."

"I don't get this," Bill English said. "Maybe you ought to begin at the beginnin'. Why should we have saved ourselves the trouble?"

"You ain't heard of Brad Winters?" the stranger queried, surprise on his face.

"No. Is that your handle?" Red asked.

The stranger laughed hollowly, and words began to pour out half hysterically: "I'm Ed Marks. Brad Winters owns the Rail W, the biggest layout this side of the mountains. He was here before they turned the country into a reservation for the Navajos, over twenty years ago. The government gave him a perpetual title to his land. They say he's had things pretty much his own way these last twenty years, leasin' ten times the graze he had under fence from the Indians. Now that they've cleared out, he thinks all this range is his. Antelope Creek, right where we're holed up, is the choicest grass in four hundred miles."

Bill English was frowning. "Then it was a bunch of these Winters riders that left you back there last night with that barb-wire harness?"

Ed Marks shrugged, more sober now and wincing with pain as he lifted his shoulders. "It was pretty dark, and I couldn't tell for sure. I'd know 'em if I ever heard one of 'em talk again, though."

Red leaned over and stared pointedly across at this partner. "Did I say something about there bein' a joker in this, Bill?"

His partner didn't answer, and for a good five minutes the three rode on in silence. Then English queried: "If this Winters wanted that Antelope Creek graze, why didn't he stake it out and file on it himself?"

"He didn't think anyone'd have the guts to come in and take it away from him," Marks explained. "No one in this country would, that's sure. It's only strangers like us, who'd never heard of Winters, that could have done it. When he got

105

around to it, it was too late. Hell, up in Colorado we read about this homesteadin' six months ago. Orndorff sold his outfit up there and hauled everything he owned, even his crew, in here with him. And he ain't the only one. There's you, and a few more."

"We just happened into it at the right time," Red Bone said. "You say there's others?"

"There's the Reeveses, John Reeves and his daughter and his brother Henry. They've had a tough time, even without bein' bothered by this Winters business. Henry Reeves has heart trouble, bad. The doctor rides up there twice a week from town. They're right above your place on the same side of the creek. We're farther up, on the other bank."

The trail was dropping down a gradual slope with the town sprawled directly ahead. It was like many other Arizona towns, a treeless slipshod cluster of buildings, for the most part adobes. Small single-room native houses fringed the town, their yards littered untidily, frame outbuildings and corrals making an unsightly background. Farther in, a few larger adobes boasted neat rectangular yards with here and there a bush or stunted tree's greenness in strange contrast to the drab browns that matched the color of the soil. At the town's center, flanking the two intersecting streets, the tarred flat roofs of stores glistened brightly in the sun's hot glare. The town's biggest and most imposing structure, the three-story hotel someone had named the Longview House, was so massive as to dwarf its neighbors and give the onlooker the impression of a hen with her chicks gathered about her at feeding time. The Longview House had clearly been built by a man with ideas too big for this country, where nine out of ten travelers would choose the hard ground and a single blanket for a bunk rather than the spacious luxury of large rooms and an iron bed with a soft mattress upon it.

"Maybe it wouldn't hurt for you to make a call on the sheriff first thing, Marks," Bill English said.

Ed Marks gave a mirthless chuckle. "That's another thing. Brad Winters elected his own sheriff. A hell of a lot of help he'd be! Gents, we're in for a tough time. As for Orndorff, he'd walk ten miles on his hands to buy himself out of trouble. He may load his things into his wagons and pull out of the country after what's happened."

"What about the others, the Reeveses?" Red queried.

"John Reeves looks like a fighter. But what good will he be with a sick man and a girl on his hands? My guess is he'll pull out, too."

Red Bone looked at English, grinning. "That sort of leaves it up to us, then, friend. You reckon we ought to hightail and get clear of this thing before it blows up under us?"

Bill English gave a grunt of derision and disgust and slapped the reins to the team. He and Red had had their share of trouble before and he doubted that it had ever occurred to Red Bone, any more than it had to him, to run at a time like this.

II

As English took the team at a trot into the intersection of Buffalo Springs' two streets, a man leaning idly against an awning post in front of the saloon on the corner called back over his shoulder to three others in the saloon doorway: "Those Antelope Creek rats have grown a lot bigger since I last saw 'em."

The words were spoken loudly enough to be heard distinctly above the rattle of the wagon's iron-tired wheels and the creak of the harness. Bill English heard them and understood immediately the insult that lay behind them.

"That's one of the bunch I met last night," Ed Marks said softly.

Pulling the team to a halt, directly at the middle of the intersection, Bill English looked back at the speaker. Then, handing the reins to Marks, he climbed lithely off the seat and sauntered across toward the saloon. Red Bone climbed down into the dust, too, cursing under his breath at having left his Colt .38 in the cabin.

English didn't halt until he stood ten feet out from the edge of the plank walk, directly facing the man who had called out the insult. This stranger was a swarthy, stockily built man with an unshaven face blackened by a week's growth of beard. He hadn't moved from his indolent, cross-legged stance against the awning post, although the three others at the saloon door had stepped closer in behind him. He wore two guns, slung low at his thick thighs. Although he smiled, the hard quality in his pale blue eyes took any hint of mirth out of his expression.

Bill English knew this breed of man, and what he said was prompted by sheer instinct. "Somethin' around here stinks. Don't they ever sweep off the walks in this town?"

He was ready for exactly what happened. Without the slightest change of expression, the man at the awning post suddenly pushed himself erect and stabbed both his hands toward holsters. Bill English took a quick, sideward step and his own right hand arced downward and up in a flashing gesture that planted his .45 hip high. As the weapon settled into line, the burly stranger's hands stopped their upward swing, his twin pearl-handled guns not yet clear of leather. In the brief silence that followed, his glance was touched by a real look of fear. A moment ago he had been cocked for trouble, chin thrust forward, knees bent. Now, held that way as if by a quick paralysis, he had a ridiculous look.

"Go ahead," English drawled. "Make your play, brother."

A man directly behind the bearded stranger made a furtive move. Bill English could see only his moving elbow. Swinging his gun a fraction of an inch to one side, English thumbed back the Colt's hammer and snapped a shot at that small target. The gun blast roared to wipe out the town's silence, and, as its echo faded, the man back there screamed and walked into view with his left hand clamped to his right elbow, his fingers red-smeared with blood. The bearded man let his weapons fall back into leather and slowly raised his hands, panic deepening in his eyes.

English, hearing the scrape of Red Bone's boots behind him, said: "Get their irons, Red."

Bone stepped onto the walk, approached the bearded stranger, and gingerly lifted the pair of pearl-handled Colts from their holsters. Then, stepping wide of the trio at the rear, he came in behind them and relieved them of their six-guns. Far down the walk, a crowd was beginning to gather.

Suddenly the swinging doors of the saloon burst outward and an oldster wearing a sheriff's five-pointed star and holding a blunt-nosed .45 in his hand stepped out onto the walk. At a glance he took in the four men in front of him, particularly the one with the wounded arm, and Bill English.

His weapon swung around and lined at English and he said sharply: "Drop that hog-leg, stranger! You're under arrest!"

He hadn't seen Red Bone, who had moved to one side of the doorway. On the heel of the sheriff's words, Bone stepped in alongside him and reached out and with a quick stab of his arm knocked the lawman's weapon down and twisted it out of his grasp.

"Easy, Sheriff," Red said. "We're only havin' our mornin's fun."

The lawman was frail-bodied, not even as tall as Red, who lacked half a head of measuring up to Bill English. He took one quick look at Red, then at English, and said, his tone a shade milder: "There's a law against shootin' up this town! What're these two doin', Folds?"

The bearded man answered without looking behind him. "I don't know yet. This one out here is pretty slick with an iron. I'd like a look at him without one."

His remark brought a thin smile to English's lean countenance. Bill nodded to his partner. "Keep an eye on 'em, Red," he said, holstering his weapon. He unbuckled his shell belt and swung it and his six-gun across onto the walk.

It was a plain invitation that the bearded Folds didn't ignore. His ugly, wicked face took on a leering smile. As he stepped down off the walk, he muttered: "I'm goin' to like this!" He came on, his steps short and choppy, until he stood a scant ten feet away.

From out on the street at the wagon, Ed Marks called: "Watch out, Bill! He can break a man's back with his bare hands! I found that out . . ."

Bill English didn't hear the rest, for he was lunging quickly to one side as Folds rushed in at him. He saw a whipping right fist coming squarely at his face and turned barely in time to roll with the blow and take it on his shoulder. It threw him off balance, and, before he could get out of the way, Folds's long, thick arms were closing about his waist.

As those bunched muscles closed vise-like about him, English thought he had lost. Then, out of sheer instinct, he threw his legs from under him and fell backward. The sudden pull of his weight rocked Folds forward. As he felt himself going down, he let go with one arm, trying to break his fall, and in that split second Bill English was rolling from his grasp.

Folds made a last futile effort to kick English with his spurred boot as he dodged clear. Bill reached out and caught a hold on that boot and twisted it, hard. Folds stumbled on his one leg, and all at once Bill let go the foot and stepped in close, driving his two fists at Folds's face. They connected with the man's bearded jaw with the force of two hard-driven hammers. Folds's head jerked first to one side, then the other, and his arms groped wildly in front of his head as he stepped back and shook his head to clear his reeling senses.

As those hands went up, English stepped to one side and slammed in a hard, chopping blow at Folds's chest. The breath left the man's lungs in a quick, gusty sigh and his face was abruptly contorted with pain. Then, as he struck out feebly to hit English, he saw his mistake and tried to raise his arms and shield his head once more. He was too late. English's fist traveled through an arc of less than a foot but it had all the drive of his flat muscles behind it as it caught Folds at the base of his jaw, alongside his right ear. Folds went down like a pole-axed steer, hitting on his suddenly loosened knees, falling forward in the lax-muscled sprawl of an unconscious man.

From the walk, Red drawled: "How'd you like that, Sheriff?"

Up the walk one of the onlookers laughed raucously until someone spoke a quick word that silenced him.

Mart Beeson, sheriff of Antelope County, swallowed hard. "Now I don't want no trouble with you two," he said warily.

"Hell, what do you call this?" Red asked. Then, motioning to the trio ahead of him on the walk: "These gents prodded us into this. Your friend Folds made a play for his iron. Wouldn't you say, offhand, that they built this fight?"

Beeson was an ineffectual man, holding office more as a figurehead for Brad Winters than for any real authority he possessed. His corn-silk mustache hid a weak mouth, and now, without a gun to back his authority, he was his real, spineless self.

"If you say that's the way it was, you must be right." He tried to brace himself with a severe look at the three men grouped near the edge of the walk, all three Brad Winters's riders. "I've told you boys you weren't to rawhide strangers."

"Wouldn't it be a good idea to lock 'em up, Sheriff?" English said quietly.

Beeson hesitated, with the obvious discomfort of a man torn between duty and fear. He wasn't forgetting the shock he'd had a minute ago— seeing Lew Folds sag into the dust. Nor was he forgetting the ease with which this sorrel-thatched stranger had taken his weapon away less than two minutes ago. So now he glared at the crowd up the walk. With a sly wink at Brad Winters's riders, he said in a loud voice: "No one can shoot the law to hell around this town! Jerry, you and Lead and Toad get on down to the jail."

English and Red Bone carried Lew Folds to the lock-up. Beeson made good his play by taking the gun Red returned to him and herding the other three before him down the street.

At the jail, a dirty, dark stone building that squatted directly alongside the massive structure

114

of the three-story hotel, Beeson made the pretense of locking the Winters riders into one of the two cells. His mistake was in leaving his bunch of keys dangling from the lock of the steel door. While the sheriff had his back turned and was trying to explain things to Red, who had handed over the prisoners' guns, Bill English reached out and quietly lifted the keys out of the lock and put them in his pocket.

Outside, meeting the lawman's show of affability with assurance that he and Red would give Buffalo Springs' laws no more trouble, Bill tossed the keys into a rain barrel to one side of the jail door. He kept talking in a voice loud enough so that Beeson didn't hear the splash. Then, turning to Red, he said: "Let's get Marks to the doctor and then load up that wire and start home."

The next two hours were an eternity of time for Sheriff Mart Beeson. He wanted to get down to the jail to let Folds and the other Winters riders out of that dark damp cell, but he couldn't summon the nerve. Red Bone stood under the awning of the general store, across the street from the jail and a few buildings below. Red was leaning against an awning post, smoking, as though he were just idling away some time, but Beeson had the feeling that the sorrel-thatched cowpuncher was watching him every second. Finally Red and English drove their wagon out of town. It was a different wagon and a different team, for Bill English had been to the feed barn and made a good trade. Beeson only casually noted that a third man, one with bandages about his head, accompanied them. At any other time he'd have been curious to know the reason for those bandages. But now he waited impatiently until the wagon was out of sight, and then ran down the street and into the jail.

He hurried through the office and into the cell-block. Folds was shouting angrily and the sheriff tried to placate him. "Now, listen, Lew," he said anxiously, "I did the best I could. Them two just left."

"You let 'em get away?" Folds raged. He looked out between the bars with a killing anger flaring in his eyes. His lips were cut and swollen and he had a lump the size of a sage hen's egg below his ear. "Beeson, you'll play hell talkin' yourself out of this with Winters."

The sheriff was a thoroughly frightened man. He came up to the cell door with hands shaking and fumbled at the lock for his keys.

They weren't there. At first he wasn't sure, so he lit a match and looked again, then scanned the floor. Finally he peered in at Lew Folds. "Which one of youse got the keys?" he asked.

"You locked us in," one of Folds's men said. "You took 'em out with you."

"I left the whole bunch right here," the sheriff

protested. "If you'd felt around, you could have turned yourselves loose."

There was more argument, with Folds's rage mounting until it was white-hot. Beeson got a lantern and made a thorough search of the jail, then of his office. Finally, when Folds bellowed for someone to get him a gun so that he could blow out the sheriff's brains, Beeson got his own gun and tried to shoot the lock apart. But whatever blacksmith had forged the iron that went into that lock had done a thorough job. The bullets ricocheted around the room until finally Folds, so impotent with rage he could hardly speak, said hoarsely: "Get a blacksmith and chisel the thing loose."

It took the blacksmith three-quarters of an hour to knock the rivets off the lock and break it. The *clang* of his hammer and chisel on the iron grating set up an inferno of sound that almost deafened the impatient prisoners. Finally they walked out of the cell. Beeson had two minutes before he made an excuse to run an errand and was nowhere to be found.

They got their guns off the sheriff's battered desk in the office and rode directly out of town. When they came to the forks in the trail that led off to Antelope Creek, Folds reined in and had a long look to the north. But finally he grunted— "We'll tell the boss about this first."—and from there on he held his black gelding to a killing run that left the animal shaking and badly blown when they finally rode into the ranch yard.

Folds went directly to the house and found Brad Winters there, in the corner of the main room where he had his desk. The rancher was kneeling before his safe, leafing through some papers, his back to the door as Folds came in. But he recognized his ramrod's boot tread and said without looking around: "Lew, you know where I put the receipt for that last feeder shipment we made last fall?"

"To hell with receipts, Brad! Listen to this!" Folds quickly told his story, all of it, for Brad Winters was a man hard to mislead.

III

When his foreman had finished, Winters took the swivel chair behind his desk and lit a cigar. He had a hawkish, grizzled face that rarely changed its hard set to betray any inner thought or emotion, and his piercing black eyes, now staring at Folds, didn't give even a hint of what he was thinking. His outfit was one of somber black except for his white shirt. He always dressed immaculately, and despite the rock-like quality of hardness to his visage it was plain that Brad Winters had grown soft with easy living. His face was more gray than tan, and his front was ample, showing evidence of an old man's paunch.

Winters had come here a man who could outride and outfight any rider in his crew, a man who was highly respected. If his boundaries had stayed open, so that he'd had to fight the natural enemies of all cowmen—squatters and rustlers—Brad Winters would have been a different man than he was today. But with his ranch surrounded by the reservation, having unlimited range at a low lease cost available from the Indians who were his friends, Winters had gradually grown soft with success and an over-easy life. His herds now numbered ten times the count any other ranch the Rail W's size could have boasted. In fact, not many of his steers were inside his own fence, and Antelope Creek was the choicest graze outside his wire, graze he had come to think of as his own. He now inwardly cursed his own negligence in not having sent his crew in to Buffalo Springs to file on that land the day the reservation had been opened to homestead. But, having accepted this circumstance, he still thought of Antelope Creek as his own, and the people settled on it now as squatters.

Lew Folds had grown tired of waiting for his answer. Now he said impatiently: "Say the word, and I'll take half a dozen men up there and gun those people out o' the country."

Winters's thin-lipped mouth curved down in a

119

sneer. "Give you the word, Lew, and you'd do me more harm than ten bad winters." He regarded his foreman with restrained anger. "That was a fool play today, Lew. Remember what I told you?"

"You said all the rules were off, that we were to make it so damned miserable for that bunch they'd pull out."

"And I said not to come out in the open with it. Like last night. That rider of Orndorff's would never have known who left him there if you hadn't forced your hand in town today."

"I didn't like the looks of them other two," Folds growled. "I still don't. Sooner or later I'll beat their brains out with my gun barrel."

Winters nodded solemnly. "You've got my permission to do that . . . providing no one sees you. But don't make town the place to pick your fights. There's too many who'll watch you. Get it into your skull, Folds, that, if we bring this out into the open, we may have a federal marshal on our necks. The government will back these homesteaders."

Folds's thick shoulders lifted in an impatient shrug. "Can you think of a better way?"

"One a lot better. Tonight you and a few others go out and pull down as much of that fence as you can before sunup. Get clear of that country before mornin'."

"They'll know who did it. That's sure bringin' it into the open."

"They'll know, but they won't be able to prove it. On the way in, swing across into the breaks and lose your sign. No federal marshal can prove a thing on us."

Folds had been frowning, but now that frown gradually gave way to a slow, broad grin. "I get it. Do anything they can't prove on us."

Winters nodded with a smug, complacent expression on his hard face.

An hour ago, as the wagon rolled into the cottonwood grove where the two partners' cabin was slowly taking shape, Ed Marks had said to Bill and Red: "Tonight'll be the time to see Orndorff and the Reeveses. Takin' a good look at me, and hearin' what happened to you two today, ought to convince 'em . . . although I doubt if it does."

So they had turned the team into the small fenced pasture that flanked the trees. Red gave them a bucket of oats, and then he and English saddled their ponies. Marks rode double with Bill as they followed the creek north to John Reeves's place.

Now, riding across the broad bench where the Reeveses' tent was an orange-lighted shape behind a blazing fire against the settling dusk, Ed Marks took a long look at the figures outlined by the fire and said: "We're in luck. That big gent up there's Orndorff."

As it turned out, Knute Orndorff had come down to the Reeveses' tent late in the afternoon to ask if they had any news of Marks, who had been missing a whole day now, and he had stayed on for the evening meal. When Orndorff, a huge-statured man even taller than Bill English, saw that Marks was one of the three that rode in toward the fire, his voice boomed a relieved welcome and he fired questions so rapidly at Ed that Bill and Red had no chance to meet John Reeves or his brother and daughter.

Marks did most of the talking. While he told Orndorff about the four riders that had been waiting along the trail for him in the darkness last night, to leave him gagged and tied helplessly with barb wire, and of the fight in town today, English had his chance to study his neighbors.

John Reeves had something of the look of a soldier. He was tall, his aquiline face striking with its pointed white beard and shock of pure white hair that topped it. While Ed and Orndorff talked, John Reeves made it a point to step across and shake hands with Bill and Red.

He brought his daughter with him, saying in a low voice: "If we hadn't had a lot of trouble on our hands, I'd have been down to pay you a visit long before this. I'm John Reeves and this is Gail." He nodded toward a chair on the other side of the fire. "That's Henry over there." The blanket-wrapped, frail-looking figure seemed strangely out of place at a campfire.

Gail Reeves was as cordial as her father, and immediately insisted that they stay for supper. She looked at Bill and said: "That is, if you'll make the coffee. Men are always better cooks than women, although they won't admit it."

Red helped her with the biscuits while Bill brewed the coffee, hardly able to take his eyes from the girl. Now that she had stepped well into the light of the fire, Bill saw instantly that Gail Reeves was a woman rare in any man's experience. She was tall, her graceful figure holding just a suggestion of boyish angularity. Her face, with its finely chiseled features, was a softer image of her father's, her eyes a deep brown and unfathomable and her hair a gold Bill English thought was the exact shade of ripe wheat.

Once she turned abruptly and happened to catch his intent inspection, and Bill saw a tinge of color mount to her cheeks. He was immediately embarrassed, and for long minutes he didn't look her way again.

He was jerked from his preoccupation as Henry Reeves's high-pitched voice called irritably: "English, we're talking to you!"

"What is it?" Bill pushed the half-gallon coffee pot into the coals and stood up, aware now that he'd ignored what was going on around him.

Henry Reeves had the look of an invalid. He

sat close by the fire, as though the warmth of the blankets wasn't enough against the gathering chill of the evening. His thin, almost gaunt face was drawn and pale. In his deep gray eyes now lay a brightness that was the only thing that seemed really alive about him, a brightness that was a clear sign of anger.

"Orndorff and I say that you had no business forcing that fight in town today," he snapped abruptly. "You're mighty careless how you mix our trouble with yours!"

Bill looked at Ed Marks and caught the man's perplexed and bewildered frown. Ed shrugged his shoulders, as if he wanted English to understand that what was taking place was beyond control.

English hadn't been listening to the conversation. Now he regretted it. All he could think to say was: "There's things a man can't take. One of them is to be called a creek rat."

Orndorff's voice boomed out of the shadows beyond Henry Reeves. "You two have spoiled it for the rest of us. We could have settled our differences with Winters peaceably. Now you've made him think we're with you in buckin' him. We're not! I didn't come to this country to spend the rest of my life with a gun in my hands, fightin' another man's fight!"

It was strange to hear such words from a man whose very look was one of towering strength. Bill English retorted bitingly: "You'd stand by and let him crowd you out of your legal rights?"

"No, we wouldn't!" Henry Reeves blazed. "But we wouldn't take to guns like a pack of cheap saddle bums! The day for guns is past."

"Easy, Henry," John Reeves put in, his expression one of shocked surprise. He turned to Bill English. "Henry doesn't know what he's saying. I apologize for him."

"The hell I don't!" his brother cried, ignoring his niece's presence. "I say this man English has made a fool's play! No apology's needed!"

"You're makin' some big talk," Red Bone put in.

"I'd make it bigger if I could move out of this chair!" Henry Reeves shouted, gripping the arms of his chair and leaning forward, white-faced, blunt-jawed, to stare coldly at English and Bone.

"Let's get out o' here," Red drawled, realizing as English did the futility of continuing the argument.

"The sooner the better!" Henry Reeves declared.

As Red stepped away from the fire, toward the spot where they'd ground-haltered the horses, Bill English looked across at the girl. Her oval face was pale, and her brown eyes mirrored a look of helpless chagrin. He felt curiously heartened to realize that she felt the same as her father.

There was nothing more to say. Orndorff had moved closer in to Henry Reeves's chair, the blunt set to his square jaw making it plain that he sided with the sick man. There was nothing Bill could do but lift his shoulders in a resigned shrug and follow Red.

As they swung into their saddles, Ed Marks's shape came up out of the darkness. "It's worse than I thought," he said in a low voice. "Orndorff's a stubborn man, hard to push. I'm damned sorry it turned out this way."

"Forget it, Ed," Bill said. "Nothin' may ever come of this."

"If it does, you two come up after me. I'm not gettin' rich workin' for that pig-headed Dutchman, and it wouldn't take a hell of a lot to make me draw my wages and pull my stakes."

"Maybe we're spooked over nothin'." Bill reined away. "But we'll let you know if we need you, Ed."

Neither of them said much until they were a good mile below the Reeves place, although Red was muttering under his breath. "The Ladies Aid missed a good bet in not makin' Orndorff a member," he declared scornfully.

English made no reply but rode on in silence. Some real and deep instinct for scenting trouble made him swing away from the creek two miles farther on. "Let's have a look at the fence on the way home," he told Red.

They came to the end of their fence and followed it on the outside, English leading the way and intending to cut in toward their cabin below, where he remembered they had left a gap in the wire that was to become a gate when it was finished. A scant 100 yards before they would have come to that gap and headed toward the cabin, a sudden clattering of hoofs far ahead brought them up tensely in their saddles.

English was the first to ram his spurs into his pony's flanks as that ominous sound reached him. The animal lunged ahead into a hard run, Red swinging in behind. For 100 rods English held a killing pace, seeing to one side of him that the fence posts were lying on the ground with a tangle of wire running brokenly between.

All at once a dim, moving shape loomed up out of the darkness ahead. As he drew the gun at his thigh, English made it out as a horse and rider, the man bent low in the saddle. He whipped up his weapon, took careful aim, and squeezed the trigger. The solid bark of his .45 was muffled by his pony's hoof clatter. As he breathed the sharp tang of powder smoke into his lungs, he saw the rider sway in the saddle. The man's hand reached out and he caught himself as he started to fall. Then, lurching back into the saddle, he suddenly reined his pony obliquely out from the line of the fence, and, before English could follow, he had disappeared into the darkness at a hard run.

Later, when they pulled in and listened to the far-off, fast-fading hoof thunder, English and Red Bone rode back and had a look at their fence. A good mile of it was down, the three strands of wire neatly cut midway between each post and the posts themselves pulled out of their holes.

"There goes a week's work, feller," Red drawled.

"They're headed south," English said. "Then the Rail W must lie off there. You sleepy, Red?"

"I'm always a little sleepy."

"Too sleepy to take a little ride?"

Red grinned unseen into the darkness. "I can always get my rest sittin' up."

IV

Brad Winters was awakened at a little past three the next morning by someone beating at his window. A cautious man always, the first thing he did was to reach under his pillow. But even as he climbed from bed and pulled on his trousers, the weapon in his hand, he knew that his precaution was unnecessary. Reflected on the window's dirty panes was a rosy glow of light that didn't have its origin in the faint gray flush of the early dawn showing in the east. Before he even reached the window and threw it open, to see Lew Folds's squat shape in the shadows outside, he knew that it was a fire.

"Take a look, Brad!" Folds shouted, pointing along the length of the house. "The barn, those two stacks of hay behind, and the wagon shed."

Winters leaned out the window and had his

look, seeing the barn take shape through fifty-foot-high sheets of flame. "Who kicked over the lantern?" he demanded in a voice that would have at any other time made Lew Folds cautious in his answer.

But Folds had come in from a hard ride two hours ago and, being waked at this time of the morning, had set his unruly temper on edge. "No one kicked over a lantern!" he blazed. "That fire was set. How the hell would it jump that hundred feet from the barn to the wagon shed if it hadn't been?"

Even before his ramrod finished, Brad Winters guessed something of what had happened. He leaned down and stepped out through the window, giving sharp orders: "Put every man you can spare into the saddle. Head north and beat 'em to the fence."

"That's what I tried to do, only the corrals are empty. Toad heard the bronc's bein' driven away and ran down there. They were gone before he could stop 'em. Brad, it's those two homesteaders!"

Winters, for once in his life, was as helpless as a man without a crew or without a horse. After he walked down to the barn, irritably seen that his men formed a bucket-line from the well house and were unsuccessfully trying to put out the fire at the saddle room in the wagon shed, he called the cook out of the line and told him to get some coffee on.

Later, when the fire was out and the layout turned ugly and bare by the first strong light of dawn, he herded his men into the bunkhouse and had the cook feed them their breakfast.

It was while Winters was sitting there at the head of the table, drinking his black coffee in a brooding silence, that a rider pounded in toward the layout. Folds got off the bench at the foot of the table and went to the door and looked out. "Up here, Mike!" he called, as the hoof drum of a hard-ridden horse faded out in the direction of the corral.

Almost immediately there was the sound of a man running toward the bunkhouse, and in another moment Mike Chavis appeared in the doorway, his dark half-breed face soberly set, bathed with perspiration. He was too breathless from his running to speak, and his Levi's and shirt were dusty.

Winters, remembering that Chavis had for the past week ridden fence along the north boundary, said crisply: "Well, what happened up your way?"

When the cowpuncher got his wind, he blurted: "North fence. Two miles of it down! That herd of two-year-olds is driftin' out toward the breaks."

Winters got to his feet. "Get your men out there, Folds!" he barked. "It's only three miles to the breaks, and, if they ever get in there, we'll spend the next two months roundin' 'em up." Every man on the crew knew he prized that herd more highly than any other stock about the place.

"How we goin' to ride without saddles or jugheads?" Lew Folds demanded.

"Take Chavis's pony and go after the stuff that was driven out of the corral this morning," Winters snapped. Then, when the ramrod hesitated: "I mean now, Folds!"

For the next few hours the crew kept out of Brad Winters's sight as well as they could, knowing the man's temper. Finally Folds drove four broncos over the crest of the hill that backed the corrals and some of the crew went out to rope them while a few more ran to the well house to drag out three long-forgotten and worn-out saddles that were in the storeroom there. In another quarter hour five riders left the layout at a hard run, headed north.

Folds wasn't one of them. He came to the house, into the big room where Winters sat at his desk. He closed the door quietly behind him, expecting the outburst that immediately came.

"You were in your bunk when that fire started!" Winters blazed out at him. "I thought I told you to spend the night pullin' down fence. Instead of that, *our* fence is pulled down, the layout burned, and our bronc's driven off. What the hell kind of a straw boss are you?"

"We was up there, doin' as you said," Folds

defended himself. "We had a mile of fence down when them two showed up out of nowhere and gunned us off the place."

"Why didn't you stay and fight? It was your chance to get rid of them for good."

Folds's blunt face took on a stupid look. "It all happened pretty quick. One of 'em took a shot at Bill Stanley and busted his arm. I sent him straight for town. I didn't know how many there were." He went on trying to make his excuses.

Winters, with a wave of his hand, commanded his ramrod to silence. "You and I'll ride up there today and offer to buy out that crew. Everyone but English and Bone. We'll settle with them later. If we throw a good scare into the others, they may leave."

"Reeves looks like a fighter. And I'd like to meet Orndorff without a man or two around to back him."

"Reeves has a sick man and a girl on his hands. I can bring him around. And I've seen bigger gents than Orndorff who'd back down. It's worth a try, Folds."

At eleven that morning Gail Reeves rode into the clearing where Bill English was working. Red Bone had left five minutes before for the edge of the cottonwoods, carrying a Winchester. "Just to make sure they don't send a bushwhacker up here for a try at us," he had said grimly.

Bill was peeling logs. He laid down his axe and walked out to meet the girl, noticing at once that her chestnut horse was badly blown. When she was close enough so that he could catch the sober, unsmiling expression on her face, he knew that something had happened.

"Howdy," he said. "Something wrong?"

"It's Uncle Henry," she told him breathlessly. "He's worse today. Dad left early for Orndorff's, and I'm all alone. Would it be asking too much for you to go up and stay at the tent while I ride to town for the doctor?"

"Sure," Bill said, only faintly surprised at the news. "But you stay and let me go to town."

Gail shook her head. "I can tell the doctor what's wrong. You can't. Otherwise, he might bring the wrong medicine."

"Go ahead," Bill said, starting across to the lean-to where his sorrel was stabled. "I'll head right up there."

"Wait!" she called, in a tone that immediately brought him around to face her once more. "I want to apologize for what Uncle Henry did to you last night. I . . . I don't want you to think Dad and I are so ungrateful."

"I knew how you felt," English told her.

She ignored his assurance and went on: "My uncle hasn't been himself lately. He and Dad came out here to make a new start, after a bank failure at home left them both poor men. In the

133

old days he'd have wanted to be with you in this fight. I hope you'll believe that."

"I do," Bill assured her quietly. "Don't worry about it."

The girl's relieved smile held a measure of gladness that quickened Bill English's pulse. Then, as he looked at her, something in the intensity of his glance brought a quick tide of color to her oval face, and without another word she wheeled the chestnut and rode out of the clearing, downcreek.

It took Bill less than twenty minutes to make that ride to the Reeveses' tent. He ground-haltered the sorrel near the cold ashes of last night's fire, and walked to the tent, and swung open the flap.

"Gail sent me up here to . . ." He broke off abruptly.

His eyes, focusing to the half light of the tent, saw something that made him check his words. Henry Reeves lay with his head and upper body sprawled loosely on a cot at the back wall, his legs and feet downslanted to the board floor in a sagging, lifeless way that made English step quickly across and take his wrist in his hand.

Reeves's body was already cold, his eyes open and staring sightlessly at the canvas above him. Bill English closed the dead man's eyes, lifted the feet onto the cot, and pulled a blanket up over his head.

Riding away from the tent, he was numbed for

long minutes by the shock of what he had found. At first he didn't know what to do, but then instinctively he knew that he must ride after Gail Reeves and break this news to her.

If English hadn't been so stunned at this swift and unexpected stroke of death, he might have been wary enough to scan the rolling open range to the west. As it was, he missed seeing the two riders that were coming in at a stiff trot toward the bench where the Reeveses' tent sat whitely against the green of the willows on the far bank.

Lew Folds saw English as he rode away and immediately reined in on his played-out bronco. "Hold on, Brad! There goes English!"

Winters pulled up, watched English until he dropped out of sight behind the screen of leaves down the trail. "Let him go," he said finally. "We'll finish our business with Reeves."

"I could swing down ahead of him and let him have it now," Folds muttered, slapping the stock of a Winchester that rode under his thigh in a saddle scabbard.

"That can come later." Winters clucked his black into motion once more and they rode directly to the tent.

After calling loudly and getting no answer, they entered the tent. Winters saw the shape on the bed, and, stepping over, he pulled the blanket down far enough to have his look at Henry Reeves's stony face.

"Dead," he muttered as Lew Folds took off his hat in a respectful gesture that seemed strange in a man of his caliber. "He must have been the sick one. You said it was heart trouble?"

Folds nodded. "Doc Macom has been comin' up here two or three times a week."

"And Bill English just rode out of here," Winters breathed. Suddenly he wheeled on his ramrod. "You know what this means?"

Folds could only stare stupidly at the rancher, not grasping what lay behind the words. But an instant later he knew, for Winters reached his right hand in under his lapel and brought out his short-barreled Colt .38 from his shoulder holster. He cocked it, and, as it fell into line with Henry Reeves's temple, he drawled: "English doesn't know it yet, but he just murdered a man."

Bill English was riding across the intersection of Buffalo Springs' two streets late that morning headed for Doc Macom's house at the far edge of town. Looking toward the bank, he saw Sheriff Beeson abruptly step into view out of the doorway, a double-barreled shotgun half raised to his shoulder.

"Reach for the sky, English!" the sheriff called.

English's muscles came taut, and he was ready to throw himself out of the saddle when Beeson called out another warning: "Take a look behind you!"

Slowly English's glance left the lawman and swung to the opposite side of the street. Lew Folds stood there in the shadow of a broad wooden awning, two six-guns in his hands lined squarely at English.

There wasn't any choice here. Bill put up his hands. Ten minutes later he had been relieved of his gun and was occupying the cell next to the one that had yesterday held Lew Folds and his riders. Neither Beeson nor Folds would talk. Bill asked them once why he was being arrested, and Folds replied curtly: "Murder, among other things."

Later, Bill thought he heard Gail Reeves's voice sounding through the heavy oak door that closed off the sheriff's office from the jail. But he couldn't be sure.

He tried not to worry, but now that he was alone and able to look back soberly over the events of the past thirty-six hours he wasn't at all sure that he would ever step out of the jail alive. For two lone men, he and Red Bone had done considerable damage on their ride last night—enough so that Brad Winters could lodge half a dozen charges against them even though he lacked adequate proof. And proof probably wouldn't be held too important. Finally, with the resignation of a man who knows the futility of worry, he lay down on the cell's creaky bunk and closed his eyes. He was asleep in two minutes.

V

The Longview House, Buffalo Springs' one hotel, seen up closely was a dilapidated relic of better days. Yet even in the darkness its three stories towered above the neighboring squat stone jail to the west and the harness shop to the east in a still regal majesty. From its top floor a man could see all the way to the hazy horizon in every direction, on clear days a good forty miles. Because of this view the original owner had run a wide-roofed balcony around the four sides of the building on a level with the top floor, painted it white. His best-paying guests were lodged in the rooms opening on it.

Tonight, as Red Bone climbed gingerly to the balcony by the none-too-steady ladder at the back of the building, he was reminded faintly of the Lincoln County courthouse, which he'd once seen and which had a balcony something like this. Ed Marks climbed up after Red and walked with him around to the front so that they could get a good look down the street toward the saloon. They'd left their ponies a good quarter mile out of town and walked in, not wanting to be seen.

Ed had ridden down the creek trail that afternoon to tell Bill and Red that Henry Reeves was dead, that John Reeves had found him, and come up to Orndorff's for some lumber to nail up a coffin. Red hadn't been much impressed with the news, but he was worried about Bill's absence and told Ed so. Ed was trying to help him think up some new reason for Bill's mysterious absence when Gail Reeves had ridden into the clearing. She had told Red a story that sent him at a run to the lean-to to saddle his bronco. Bill English was in jail, accused of murdering Henry Reeves, and Gail couldn't, wouldn't believe it.

"We'll decide that later," Red told her. "You can help by ridin' up for your father and gettin' him into town as quick as you can."

Just now Red didn't know why he'd sent the girl after John Reeves. If Bill English was in this kind of trouble, no one could help him. And, looking down the darkened street toward the saloon, Red knew instantly that Bill *was* in for trouble. Even though the wooden awning in front of the saloon hid what was going on in the shadow of the walk, Red could guess. The dull orange wash of the saloon lights flared out into the street time and again as the batwing doors opened and closed. In that light were outlined the grotesque shadows of moving men, many men judging by the number of horses tied at the hitch rails down there.

"That'll be Winters primin' a lynch mob," Ed Marks said softly alongside Red. "Hell, ain't there nothin' we can do?"

Red didn't answer. Instead, he glanced pointedly below to the jail roof that was directly under them. Gazing down onto that dark shadowed rectangle, Red was picturing the look of the inside of the place as he had seen it yesterday. The cells were along the street side of the big room, the steel grating of their doors directly in line with the low rock-topped partition that split the roof down the center and that he could see now in faint outline. A dozen glimmerings of hope came to him, yet faded out in the knowledge that Buffalo Springs' jail was as impregnable as a solid chunk of granite. It was of rock, fireproof, with the bars of the single small window made of two-inch steel set in concrete.

"Dynamite's the only thing that'll do the trick," Ed Marks said, reading Red's thoughts.

Red didn't know what he could do. Neither did Ed Marks. They started back along the jail side of the balcony, walking soundlessly, and were almost midway along it when a flickering light suddenly showed in one of the windows.

Red jerked to a halt and stepped backward. But before he had stepped out of view of that window, the light had strengthened. Red had a fleeting glimpse into the lighted room. He could see a thin-faced oldster with a cigar in his mouth, bending over a lamp on the top of a roll-top desk. And Red saw something else in the far corner. It was a five-foot safe, painted black, its door standing open so that he could see its thick sides and get some idea of how heavy it must be. He noted pointedly that the safe stood on castors.

He put out a hand and halted Marks. "Wait, Ed." He thought he had something. Then, reaching down to draw his gun from its holster, he went on. "You hang close in behind me. I may need help."

With that brief word he stepped in toward the window and swung his six-gun in a tight arc that broke one of the top section's four glass panes. As the shattered glass fell inward before his blow, he stuck his arm and the gun through the jagged opening and drawled: "Reach for your ears, friend!"

The man inside had whirled at the sound of the breaking glass. Now his face went pale with fear. The cigar fell from his mouth as he slowly raised his hands.

Red reached in and unlatched the window. He raised it and stepped inside, noting with satisfaction that the sill was low, only two inches above the floor. It was a big window, evidently designed to give the occupant of the room a broad vista of the rolling country.

"We're sorry about this, mister," Red drawled to the dumbfounded man. "But we want your safe, not what's in it. Ed, grab a sheet off that bed, tear it into strips, and tie up this gentleman."

"You . . . I'll have the sheriff on you two!" the oldster sputtered.

"That won't be nothin' new," Red said dryly. He'd relieved the man of a snub-nosed .38 from a back pants' pocket, and pushed him none too gently back on to the bed in one corner.

"I'm the manager here!" the oldster raged. "Mart Beeson's a friend of mine. You two won't get away with this."

"I'm beginnin' to think you're right," Red agreed. "But we'll pay for the damage we do." He stepped over to the safe, closed the door, and spun the combination. Putting his shoulder to it, he pushed. The safe moved a bare inch under all his strength.

But after Ed had bound and gagged the hotel manager, making him as comfortable as he could on the bed according to Red's instructions, the two of them together were able to move the safe halfway across the room in ten minutes' time. Red put the light out then, and told Ed what his plan was.

"It'll never work," Ed declared.

It took another twenty minutes to push the safe to the window and tilt the front legs onto the low sill. At that point Red crawled over the safe and onto the balcony and took a long look below.

"The balcony won't hold it," Ed said from inside.

Red said he thought it would. "But after we get it out, we've got to move it ten feet farther along. Let's get at it."

Red's shirt was clinging wetly to his bunched muscles and sweat was lining Ed Marks's high forehead when at last they got the safe into position. "Must weigh half a ton," Ed said as he leaned over the railing and looked down. "Think this is about right, Red?"

"Another foot."

So they moved it another foot. The timbers of the balcony floor creaked ominously.

Red took a long breath, murmured—"Watch out, Ed."—and with his feet braced against the side of the building pushed with all the strength in him. The safe tipped, the railing ahead splintered outward in a sound that might have been heard for a quarter of a mile. Then, slowly at first but with its dead weight gathering momentum, the safe toppled off the balcony and downward.

The crash of its landing shook the whole building. The safe went through the jail roof as though its timbers and two feet of earth were paper. A hollow *swoosh!* boomed up as it crashed through the floor inside the jail. A billowing cloud of dust rolled outward along the walk on the street. The far wall tottered, caved inward.

Bill's first thought, as the crash jerked him into wakefulness, was that it was an earthquake. The cot tipped and spilled him onto the floor. Dirt and rock shards sprayed down on him as he rolled onto his feet. Then the dust cleared and he saw faint starlight shining through the jagged ten-foot opening in the roof of the corridor beyond his cell. And in that light he noticed something else.

His cell door was sprung outward at the bottom where the floor had caved in, the bars bent, and the lock snapped off. In the middle of the corridor beyond the cell was a bulky, rectangular shape that had gone through the flooring, broken through its joists, and sprung the cell door.

From above came the hollow blast of a shot. Bill lunged against the bars. The sprung door had swung outward barely far enough to let him squeeze through.

"Can you make it, Bill?"

It was Red's voice, and Bill looked up and saw his friend there on the balcony.

Red was swinging up his six-gun and now thumbed another shot obliquely downward. Out on the street a man's shrill cry was an echo to the shot. A gun barked savagely from out there, and Red dodged back out of view. Boots pounded on the plank walks in front as Bill stepped up onto the safe, reached for the edge of a broken roof joist, and swung himself up through the hole.

Red stayed on the balcony until Ed Marks had descended the ladder and tossed a gun up to Bill. Then, as Red's gun ceased its low-throated roar from above, Bill English's spoke out from the parapet of the jail's front wall. He emptied his six-gun at the shadows on the walk opposite, and by that time Red was calling from the alley out back: "All set, Bill!"

Once Bill had swung down off the roof, the three of them started down the alley, Bill taking the shells Red handed him and reloading his weapon. Suddenly Bill saw an indistinct shape step into view from behind a lean-to. A powder flash outlined a man down there for a moment, and, as he felt a bullet whip past his ear, Bill thumbed a shot at that now darkened target and saw the man stumble and fall.

"What about horses?" he asked as he swung into the shadows alongside Red and Marks behind the harness shop.

"Too far out," Red said, mumbling a crisp oath. "We were afraid to bring 'em in any closer."

"Then let's get out into the street." Bill stepped into the narrow passageway between the harness shop and the hotel and edged along it toward the street.

The Rail W riders on the street were still firing at the jail. They had spread out down the walks on both sides of the building and two guns across there were sending a steady hail of lead toward the top parapet of the jail's rock wall where Bill had been half a minute ago.

Behind him, Bill English heard the sudden pound of boots in the alley and a man back there cried: "Get up onto the hotel. We'll have 'em from there!"

The three of them waited in the shadows of that passageway for almost a minute. "What do you aim to do, Bill?" Red asked as they stood there.

"Take our pick of the horses in front of the saloon," Bill answered. Red didn't see how his partner was going to do it, but he kept his doubts to himself.

Then Brad Winters's voice bellowed from high up on the far side of the hotel: "They're inside, Folds! Someone bust into the hardware store and get dynamite." No one had seen them leave the jail, and Winters's assumption was a logical one.

All they had to do was wait. Winters's men slowly closed in on the jail. Once one of them stepped so close along the walk that Bill English could have reached out a hand and tapped him on the shoulder. The man was hugging the shadows, close to the store fronts.

"Now," Bill breathed, and lunged from the darkness of the passageway.

The three of them were halfway across the street, angling down toward the now empty saloon, before a man beyond the jail shouted— "That's them! There they go!"—and whipped a wild shot after them.

As Bill jerked loose the reins of the bay horse he'd picked out, he lifted a booted foot and savagely kicked at the tie rail. It snapped in two and fell into the dust. Vaulting onto the frightened

146

pony's saddle, Bill swung the animal through the hitch rail's opening and onto the walk, beneath the awning. Red, already mounted on a black horse, wheeled and followed. The clatter of their ponies' hoofs echoed along the length of the street like an undertone in the inferno of sound that guns suddenly let loose. Ed Marks stayed in the street for twenty yards but finally ran his pony through the space between two tie posts and swung in behind them.

Bullets from the hotel balcony pounded into the awning overhead as they raced their horses down the street. Once, from the shadows across the street, a man fired point-blank at English. A hot, searing pain shot through Bill's chest as the bullet burned him. An instant later his own gun was bucking in his hand, adding its throaty chant to the others.

They were clear at last, pounding past the town's last low adobe house and out the trail into open country. English, ahead, swung wide of the trail as the far-off hoof thunder of pursuing riders shuttled out from behind. When they had covered another mile, they drew rein and listened as that mutter of pounding horses ran on past and slowly faded into the night's stillness.

"Now tell me about it," Bill said, taking the tobacco Red offered him and building a cigarette.

Red told him, and, when he was finished, Bill said: "Henry Reeves didn't have a bullet through his head when I saw him. He was dead, yes. But no one killed him."

"It could have been Folds or Winters, or both," Ed Marks said thoughtfully. "They brought the news to town, accordin' to Gail. Bill, you were framed."

"What does she think?" Bill asked, feeling the pound of his pulse in his temples.

Red chuckled. He must have understood the touch of anxiety in his friend's voice. "The same as we do, Bill. She's the one that sent us in here."

VI

They made a wide swing to the north toward Antelope Creek. All Red had had to do to make Bill English throw his spurs to his horse was to mention that Gail and her father were now quite likely riding for town. All Bill English could think of was that they might be too late to stop Gail and John Reeves from meeting the posse. Knowing what the temper of Brad Winters's men would be after the jail break, Bill wasn't so sure that hard-bitten crew would be satisfied until they'd strung up at least one homesteader.

Two miles short of Red's and Bill's cabin, as they followed the creek trail, English suddenly reined in and held up a hand. As soon as their horses stood motionlessly, Red and Ed Marks heard the muffled *thud* of horses headed toward them down the trail. Bill led them to a willow brake a scant ten yards to one side of the trail, and there they waited.

Three riders trotted their ponies into view a half minute later. It was Gail Reeves's slight figure that Bill recognized first through the darkness. The other two were her father and Orndorff. He hailed them.

Gail was obviously relieved to see them. John Reeves's look of relief matched hers. Orndorff maintained a surly silence as Bill told how Red and Ed Marks had broken him out of jail.

When Bill had finished, John Reeves said: "I can prove you didn't kill Henry, English. And here's how I can prove it."

He was about to continue when suddenly Orndorff spurred his pony close in alongside Bill and whipped a short-barreled .45 from his waistband.

"Throw 'em up, English!" he ordered. "Throw up your hands, or damned if I won't take you back to town slung across my saddle."

As Bill slowly raised his hands, the homesteader glanced across at John Reeves. "I don't have any notion of what you know, Reeves. But this man goes back to jail until this thing's settled. I'm for law and order in this country, and damned if I'll see you or anyone else try to get around that law."

He was so intent in what he had to say that his glance for a moment strayed from English. In that brief interval of time Bill kicked loose his left foot from the stirrup and lunged from the saddle. His right hand reached out and wrenched the heavy weapon from Orndorff's grip, and the force of his lunge was enough to topple the big man from his horse.

Red and Marks dismounted quickly. Red got hold of Orndorff's arms, Marks his feet.

Bill English thought a moment. Then he said: "Tie him and gag him, Red. We'll leave him here to cool off until we've got this thing settled. First thing we know he'll be puttin' his foot in it and gettin' one of us killed."

So Orndorff was unceremoniously bound hand and foot and gagged. Bill hated to do it, realizing that the man's stubbornness and belligerence were prompted only by a sincere desire to avoid trouble and the burning of gunpowder. But now he had neither the time nor the patience to reason the thing through with the man. That would have to come later.

"You started to tell me something about your brother's death," Bill said after they'd finished carrying Orndorff into the willow brake that had hid them only three minutes ago.

John Reeves did have something to say, something important, and, when he finished, Bill English had something to say, too. It took him all of five minutes to convince Reeves that what he was urging him to do was right. In the end, Reeves gave in.

A few seconds later he and Gail rode on toward town. Bill, Red, and Ed Marks also turned toward Buffalo Springs, but by the same way they had come, keeping clear of the trail.

It was only a powerful voice that saved John Reeves from being riddled by Rail W bullets that night. When he and Gail heard the posse approaching along the creek trail, Reeves made the girl ride far off to one side, into a thicket of willows that grew along the creekbank. He stayed where he was in the trail, and, when he could see the vague outline of the leader of the posse trotting his horse up the trail, he shouted as loudly as he could.

The leader heard him and drew rein. The others came up fast and stopped. Someone shouted: "Who is it? Call out or we'll open up on you!"

"It's John Reeves," the homesteader answered. "Is Brad Winters there?"

Winters's voice spoke out: "I'm here. Hold your hands over your head and ride up on us. Easy, so we'll know what you're doin'."

When they had surrounded him, Reeves said tonelessly: "I was on my way in to see how they're treatin' Bill English. If that man lives until mornin', I'll walk into that jail and kill him myself, like he killed Henry."

Winters was close enough so that Reeves caught a flicker of a smug smile on the rancher's face as he said: "You're out of luck, Reeves. English's red-headed friend broke him out of jail tonight."

John Reeves let his jaw draw open in feigned astonishment. Then he swore loudly, violently. "And you, with two dozen men and the sheriff to back you, let him get away?"

"They made a fool play and made it stick." Winters explained. "They've had all the luck so far, but my hunch is their luck is finished. We'll hunt 'em down as soon as we have light enough. Right now I'm headed up to their cabin to burn it down."

"You waste time on a thing like that while they're on the loose?" Reeves cried. "Your place is back in Buffalo Springs, roundin' up every decent man who can fork a horse."

Winters frowned thoughtfully, his expression only faintly readable in the darkness. "I hadn't thought of that," he admitted. His word didn't count too much with Buffalo Springs' citizens.

"Then it's time to be thinkin' about it," Reeves declared. "Get back to town. Call a meetin'. I'll name any man that won't ride with us a coward to his face. I want Bill English taken alive or dead by tomorrow night."

Brad Winters was plainly dumbfounded. He hadn't realized until a few seconds ago how cleverly he'd maneuvered this thing. So now he turned in the saddle and said to Lew Folds: "I told you John Reeves wasn't behind all this. We'll go back to town like he says. He's goin' to help us."

Less than an hour later, in Buffalo Springs' schoolhouse, John Reeves for the first time in his life faced an audience. It was a small one, composed of a dozen of Buffalo Springs' most representative citizens. Brad Winters, Lew Folds, and Mart Beeson were there with half a dozen hard-faced Rail W riders. Reeves had insisted that only a few men come to listen to what he had to say. These were to be the leaders of the posse that would set out as soon as he finished giving them their instructions.

The rest, some fifty more men, were busy saddling their horses out on the street or at home. The score of men here had grouped themselves along the back wall of the schoolroom, behind the desks that were too small to seat them. Reeves stood behind the teacher's desk, on the foot-high platform. As he cleared his throat to speak, he glanced toward Winters and his hard-faced men and was glad that he'd sent Gail Reeves to the hotel.

"Gentlemen," he began slowly, "early this

morning my brother Henry was alive and making a hard fight to stay alive because of a bad heart. At ten o'clock this morning he was dead with a bullet through his head. That bullet ended his slim chance of making his own fight for life. He was shot brutally and without warning as he lay on his cot in our tent up Antelope Creek. I want you to remember how he died." He paused, wiped his high forehead with his bandanna. "This morning I left the homestead and rode north to see a neighbor on business. Shortly after I left, Henry had a turn for the worse. My daughter Gail immediately started to town for the doctor. On her way she asked our nearest neighbor, Bill English, to ride back and stay with Henry until she returned. She thought she could trust Bill English."

A subdued, angry murmur ran through the group at the back of the room. Reeves paused, letting it die out before he continued. "What Bill English did from then on until the time he showed up in town, nearly two hours later, none of us knows. But we do know this. Brad Winters and Lew Folds were riding out beyond my place this morning when they heard a shot. Not knowing what it was, they came through my fence to have a look. They were in time to see Bill English riding away from my tent, a gun in his hands. He was cleaning that gun, so they say."

He held up a hand to cut off the second angry

mutter of conversation from his listeners. "Winters and Folds came directly to town and arrested English as he rode down the street. English later claimed he'd found Henry dead in the tent and that he'd come in to tell my daughter not to bother getting a doctor. That is English's story."

John Reeves paused, glanced once toward the front door to one side of the low platform on which he stood. After that single sidelong glance he went on: "Gentlemen . . . you especially, Sheriff . . . Bill English told the truth. He did find Henry dead on his cot. But he didn't find a bullet through Henry's head. I know . . . because I had come back to the tent before English arrived and saw Henry myself. He died of heart failure!"

Reeves heard the *creak* of the door hinges even before he swung around to see Bill English stepping through the front door of the room, Red Bone directly behind him. Bill's hands were at his sides, his right one within finger reach of his holstered Colt. Then Reeves swung his glance around until it rested on Brad Winters at the back of the room.

"Winters," his voice intoned levelly. "Either you or Folds shot Henry through the head after he was dead. You framed . . ."

He didn't have a chance to finish for suddenly Brad Winters lunged to one side, his hand stabbing under the lapel of his coat to his shoulder holster. That hand moved so fast that John Reeves all at once felt panic grip him. "Look out, Bill!" he cried.

But Bill English had seen the first hint of Brad Winters's move. His hand came alive in a streaking upward sweep that planted his gun hip high. Red stepped out from behind him, feet planted widely, his two hands sweeping toward his guns. Bill pulled the hammer back, released it as Winters's weapon swung into line. The two shots blended into one prolonged explosion that shook the windows, English's gun lancing its stab of flame a split second before Winters's.

Bill threw himself to the floor, aware that other guns were unholstered now. The Buffalo Springs men were frantically running toward the back door. Bill had the satisfaction of seeing Brad Winters's squat shape jerk rigidly in a stiff-kneed stagger, his gun arm dropping. With that, Bill let his glance swing around to Lew Folds, and dropped his sights onto Folds as the man thumbed back the hammer of his six-gun.

But before Bill could squeeze trigger, Red's gun cut loose to one side of him in a staccato chant of deafening explosions. Folds's big frame jerked in a spasm that all at once bent him at the waist and dropped him to the floor, head down.

The group back there broke wildly. Mart Beeson dived headfirst through the window at his elbow.

Two Buffalo Springs men followed. With a scant instant to spare, Bill threw a sure shot into the chest of a Rail W rider in the group that had instinctively crowded in around Brad Winters a moment ago. The man went backward stiffly and slumped to the floor weakly, trying to raise his weapon. One of his companions jackknifed to the floor as Red's gun spoke once more.

From the front of the room, to one side of Bill English, John Reeves shouted—"Throw down your guns!"—but his voice was drowned out as a burst of shots cut loose from a far corner by the back door where two Rail W riders were fanning their guns empty.

Swinging his weapon around on that pair, Bill English had his arm knocked down by a bullet that hit his six-gun and glanced into his right shoulder. His hand was numb as he rolled to one side to lie behind the raised platform from which John Reeves had been speaking only seconds before. He shifted his weapon to his left hand and emptied it at the pair back there, and one man sprawled into the open doorway. The second hesitated, then turned and ran.

Suddenly there was silence in the room. As Bill shucked the shells out of his weapon and dropped new loads into the cylinder, Red Bone drawled: "That's right, boys! Just drop your cutters and start huggin' your ears!"

Bill English got up off the floor just as John

Reeves rose from behind the desk that had sheltered him these last thirty seconds. Red stood with both his guns in his hands, warily eying four Rail W men in the far back corner of the room. All four had hands high above their heads. They'd been caught there, with no window or door near enough to offer them a way out. "Where's Mart Beeson?" Bill said. "He was here when this cut loose."

"He was the first one through the window." Red grinned. "If he's smart, he's halfway to . . ."

Suddenly Red saw Brad Winters's loosely sprawled figure move. At the limit of his vision, he saw Bill whip up his weapon as Winters's suddenly raised arm brought his blunt-nosed .38 into line. Winters's gun exploded and its sound was prolonged by the thunder of English's answering shot. Then a blue hole appeared at the center of Brad Winters's forehead and his head slumped on his chest, as his whole body again collapsed on the floor.

Bill, too, was down. That was the first thing Red saw as he swung about. John Reeves had reached Bill before Red realized fully what had happened. Reeves took one look, muttered: "Get the doctor, quick. I'll see to these others." Red turned and bolted for the door, for the first time in his life knowing fear.

Later, after they'd moved Bill over to the hotel to Gail Reeves's room, and the doctor had finished and stepped out into the narrow hallway, Red halted his nervous pacing to ask, hollow-voiced: "What are his chances, Doc?"

The sawbones' face was a hard one to read, inscrutable in its long-trained professional blankness. But now that face broke from its hard set and shaped a genial smile.

"If he gets plenty of that medicine, he'll pull through." He chuckled.

"What medicine?" Red demanded.

For his answer, the sawbones beckoned. Tip-toeing back along the hallway, he soundlessly opened the door to the room in which Bill English lay fighting for his life.

"That." The sawbones pointed into the room.

Gail Reeves was kneeling beside the bed, and, as Red Bone watched, she leaned over and kissed Bill's forehead.

Red closed the door and grinned with relief. "I'll have to tell Bill about that," he said. "She's takin' advantage of him." He saw then that the medico wasn't the only one present. Ed Marks, who'd been missing for the past hour and a half, stood a few feet away. Beside him loomed Orndorff's solid bulk.

The homesteader had a guilty, half-ashamed look on his square face. As he met Red's even glance, his eyes dropped. "Reckon I've made a prime fool o' myself," he muttered. "I'd give my right arm if this hadn't happened to English. It was partly my fault for not pitchin' in and helpin'."

Red shook his head slowly. "Nothin' could have changed it. But from now on things'll be your way, Orndorff, less gunpowder and more honest law."

Back-Trail Betrayal

Jon Glidden completed this story in September and on October 5, 1937 it was submitted by his agent to Street & Smith's *Western Story Magazine*. It was titled "Back-Trail Betrayal." It was purchased on December 31, 1937 and appeared in the issue dated March 26, 1938. The author was paid $202.50 upon publication.

I

Soapy waited until old Matt Byne looked up from the letter he was reading, then said complainingly: "What you waitin' for? What does he say?"

Matt was sitting behind the battered oak desk in his ranch office, Soapy across the room in a tilted chair by the window. Matt didn't answer immediately, but sat fingering his longhorn mustache with a worried frown deepening the seams on his weathered visage. Finally Soapy growled again, irritably, whereupon Matt pulled his spectacles a little lower on his hawk-like nose and picked up the letter on the desk before him. He read aloud:

Dear Soapy and Matt:

Some trouble has come up here that has me whipped unless I have money right away. I need $5,000. If you can spare it, send it with a good man who can use his guns, and have him here no later than the 28th. Beginning next Thursday, he can find me at the hotel in town. This is all I can tell you now. Betty says howdy to you both. You two stay at home—it won't do you any good to come.

Your friend,
Steve Hall

163

Soapy's old faded eyes narrowed as Matt finished, and the two of them sat in silence for a long moment. Then Matt Byne slammed a gnarled fist upon the desk top and exploded: "Get our jugheads saddled, Soapy! We're leavin' as soon as I can open the safe and get that money for Steve."

Soapy rose stiffly from his chair and hobbled across to the desk. He leaned on it, faced Matt, and said quietly: "We can't, old-timer." He reached down and tapped his right thigh. "Not me with this game leg. I couldn't straddle a hull for more'n six hours without a rest. And you're so crippled with rheumatics it hurts you just to set still in that chair. Nope, we've got to do like Steve says. Send a good man, a man who can sling his irons fast and shoot straight."

Matt's scowl faded as he realized the truth in Soapy's words. "But who'll it be?" he queried. "That's a large order with what we got to pick from."

Soapy rubbed his bearded chin, muttering thoughtfully: "It couldn't be Riley Thomas. He'd stop on the way for a drink and never get there. And Jeff Hampden's wife isn't feelin' none too good, so you couldn't drag Jeff away with a team o' mules." Abruptly his look brightened. "There's Adam Clay."

Matt nodded and muttered sourly: "Yeah, there's Clay."

"I've seen him shoot," Soapy insisted. "The

other day, when Charlie's bronc' shied at that rattler and pitched Charlie off alongside it, Clay was there and had his iron out quicker'n I could drain a glass o' red-eye. It was forty feet, but he blew the head off that sidewinder. He's our man."

Matt's frown deepened. "He may be the man, but what do we know about him? Who is he, where's he from, can we trust him? No, Soapy, we can't send Clay."

"Why? You think he holds a grudge? Maybe you did kick him and those other squatters off that north range so's you could use it, but you bought their critters at a fair price and you gave Clay a job afterward. He's been danged lucky this winter that he wasn't runnin' his own brand. He's had three squares a day and money in his pocket. The other way he'd have lost everything he had."

"I still don't trust him."

"Trust him?" Soapy queried. "Who said anything about trustin'? Now, listen, Matt. We haven't got any choice. Steve wants a man that can sling his guns. Who else is there? Adam Clay's the only man in the outfit that could hit a haystack at more'n fifty yards. I say he's the one to go and we'll just have to trust him."

"What's your plan?"

"Where is that single-barrel Greener you picked up down in old Mexico that time, Matt?"

Matt was puzzled. He nodded toward a large cupboard in one corner of the room. Soapy went over to it, rummaged around inside, and finally lifted out a dusty single-barreled shotgun. When he wiped it off with a rag, it brought out the intricate etching on the barrel and the fine carving of grip and stock. Soapy held it up and said: "You're givin' this gun to Steve, Matt. Poke the money in the barrel, along with a letter to Steve. Take the gun down and put it in a case, and send it along with Clay. He won't know what he's carryin'."

Matt was still dubious. "What if Clay finds out?"

"He won't. Now you quit the complainin' and write Steve a note and roll it up in the money and be ready in about ten minutes. I'm goin' out after Clay. What the devil, Matt, we got to do this. Clay's the only man we can send."

Ten minutes later Soapy returned with a man whose broad shoulders nearly filled the doorway. The newcomer was tall, and wore cowpuncher's Levi's, cotton shirt, and gray vest. When he moved, it was with an effortless ease that showed an animal-like quality of leashed strength. He nodded to Matt, and waited.

Matt said: "We've got the job for you, Clay. A friend of mine by the name of Steve Hall down in Wagon Fork is bein' pestered by rustlers. You're to go down there and help him. He needs a fast man with a hog-leg and we think you fit the bill. It's close onto two hundred and fifty miles and you're to get there in a hurry. From Thursday on, Steve will be waitin' for you at the hotel in Wagon Fork. He's got a daughter we both think a lot of. Don't let anything happen to 'em." Matt paused to lift the shotgun off his desk. "I'm sendin' this on down to Steve as a present. He goes turkey huntin' every fall and I've had this thing layin' around gatherin' dust for four years now. He can use it."

"Yeah," Soapy put in. "That'll take Steve's eye. Y'see, Clay, it's a gun Matt picked up down in old Mexico from a gent who didn't know what it was worth. It's from Spain, rare, one of the finest guns ever made. They're hard to find these days and better'n anything a man can get for love or money. You take good care of it."

He reached over and picked up a canvas, fleece-lined case. Then, breaking the gun, he took it apart and dropped it in the case, handing it to Adam Clay.

"I'll be on my way in five minutes," Clay said, taking the gun and going out the door.

Matt was smiling as the door closed. "You should have been a peddler, Soapy. That was a good story."

The man they called Adam Clay rode fifty-three miles before sundown. Traveling ahead of a posse on and off for four years had given him the habit of making good time in the saddle. He made a careful camp. Habit again. When he had eaten, he unlaced the shotgun case from behind the saddle cantle and opened it. He took out the damascened barrel and poked a stick down it. The three tight rolls of bills, dropping out at his feet, brought a meager smile to his face but no surprise, for a suspicious man is hardly ever surprised.

Now why would that old fool spoil a good play by tryin' to make a Greener a rare gun? he mused. He turned the gun over in his hands, recognizing markings long familiar to him. Then he took barrel and stock and tossed them far out into the brush to one side of the fire.

After counting one roll and finding it to be a little over $1,500, he whistled softly and laid it along with the others. Then he packed his pipe and considered the fire. *This is it,* he mused. *Queer how things even up.*

What made it queer to Clee Adams—for this was his real name—was that this was an easy chance of getting even with Matt Byne. Matt hadn't thought much about it nearly a year ago when he dammed up Cedar Creek and took the water away from the half dozen squatters, Clee along with the rest, who depended on the stream for their living. Matt thought he'd been big about it, offering them a fair price for their stock, and offering them all jobs. But he hadn't been fair to Clee, who was trying to get a new start in a strange country and had nearly succeeded.

That had been Clee's second failure, but he put

down his pride and took Matt's job rather than starve. Four years ago a drought, no money, a crooked sheriff, and another range hog like Matt Byne had driven him to the wall with his first small outfit, had driven him to the dark trails. This was a repetition of that experience, the details differing, the outcome the same. When a man's down, nursing a grudge, hating anybody who owns more than five horses and fifty critters, it's hard to see straight. Clee Adams didn't care about seeing straight tonight, for here was his chance to even the score with Matt Byne and crotchety old Soapy who approved of everything his friend Matt did.

Clee knew what he was going to do. The border lay seventy miles to the south, and Mexican cattle were cheap. But wait—hadn't he heard of this Steve Hall's layout down beyond the Iron Claws? He had. And Hall ran another big brand, was probably another of Matt's stripe, another grasping range hog.

He grinned with secret delight at what bobbed up in the back of his mind. Wouldn't it be nice to sink one range hog with the money stolen from another? If Steve Hall needed money before a certain day, and, if Matt Byne's didn't arrive, wouldn't the money of Clee Adams do? Once he had that toehold, it would be easy to sink an outfit—or maybe make a cleaning for himself. Thinking this, he wondered, too, why his conscience didn't bother him. This would be wrong to some men, but it was right to him. *About the rightest thing I ever did,* he breathed, almost aloud.

So that night, after smoothing the money into two bundles and putting it in two pockets of his money belt, he kept along the west trail that would take him to Wagon Fork. He rode hard all the next morning and well into the afternoon, when his roan gave out from sheer exhaustion. Clee traded the animal for a fine palomino stallion at an outfit deep in the foothills of the Iron Claws. He had two hours' sleep that night, having covered 140 since leaving Matt Byne.

Early the following afternoon he saw, far ahead, the sparse cluster of trees and buildings that was his goal. Ten minutes after sighting Wagon Fork, he saw something that seized his interest and held it more forcibly. A quarter mile ahead along the trail a chestnut horse stood outlined by the dull green of a mesquite thicket. Clee eyed the rider slouched in the saddle and, after a careful scrutiny, reached across to run the palm of his hand over the smooth butt of the Colt at his left hip.

What happened surprised Clee, for he was approaching warily. The rider ahead suddenly spurred out from the thicket and came directly toward him at a stiff trot. Clee wheeled his palomino aside, so that his gun arm was hidden, only to discover a moment later that the rider was a girl—a girl outfitted in a man's cotton shirt and Levi's, her brown hair catching the sun under the edge of her broad-brimmed hat so that it took on a copperish sheen. She sat the saddle lithely, and, as she drew closer, he felt a sudden admiration for the fine regularity of her strong face.

The girl reined in twenty feet away, holding the chestnut at a stand while she asked: "Are you the man Matt Byne sent?"

This, then, was Steve Hall's daughter. Clee knew it for a certainty, remembering Soapy's comment. He masked his recognition behind a studied blankness of his lean face and answered politely: "The way you look makes me wish I was, miss. Anything I can do?"

She forced a smile that obviously was an effort to hide her keen disappointment. "No," she said, "not unless you've got some money you wouldn't mind parting with." When she caught the momentary surprise he allowed to show in his face, she laughed and hastened to assure him: "No, there's nothing you can do. I shouldn't have stopped you like this."

Clee's smile mirrored hers and held even after she had ridden on past him and back along the trail. As he watched her receding figure, he sobered once more, for this would be the first time he had ever gone against a woman, and he wasn't liking it.

Clee Adams wore his Colt in a high-slung holster at his left thigh with the butt of the

171

weapon fronted, as his father had taught him for the cross draw. That fact, coupled with his riding the palomino, was what changed his luck.

A half hour after meeting the girl he was walking the stallion into the far limits of the single, straight street of Wagon Fork when a man standing in the doorway of a low adobe house looked out and saw him. The man's gaze clung to him for the space of five seconds, inspecting him critically. Then the watcher disappeared inside the house and a moment later came out the rear door and ran up the alley that backed the buildings along the street.

Thus, before Clee was well inside the town limits, the word had spread that a stranger wearing a butt-fronted six-gun and riding a palomino stallion had come in off the east trail. The reaction to the news varied with the men who heard it. Some stayed as they were, lounging under the awninged walk or at the tables in the three saloons of the town. Others hurried down the walks to the group that was already forming in front of the livery barn. One, an oldster a little the worse for whiskey, left the bar of a saloon, went out front, and lifted a Winchester out of the boot of a saddle that wasn't his, and took the narrow passageway between two buildings that let into an alley. Once there, he hurried to the rear of a single-story building and laboriously shinnied up a drainpipe to the roof. He ran to the front of the building, the rifle clutched in his hands.

A few seconds later Clee Adams rode into sight, his palomino at a walk as he looked along the street ahead. He had reined aside toward the livery barn door when a single sharp explosion cracked across the stillness, and a cloud of powder smoke drifted lazily from behind one corner of the false-fronted building the oldster had climbed.

Clee acted instinctively as the bullet whipped the air past his cheek. He rolled out of the saddle, lit easily on the tensed muscle of his left shoulder, and lay still with his right hand under him and closed about the butt of his still holstered weapon. He had seen that telltale bluish cloud of smoke that drifted out from the building two doors below, and now he watched the corner of its false front.

It was less than three seconds later that the oldster appeared, leaning around the corner of the flimsy partition atop the building, holding his rifle in one hand as he shouted down: "There's one for Steve Hall! Any of you gents down there want to make anything of it?"

Before the words had echoed out of hearing, Clee was rolling on his side, his six-gun streaking out in a draw that dropped the weapon into line with the man on the roof. Clee thumbed the hammer twice, already realizing that the distance was too great for accuracy. He was surprised to see the man's hold suddenly tear loose. The oldster swayed off balance a moment in his fright at the lead that had whistled past him. Then he lost his balance, toppled forward, and somersaulted through the awning to the rotten boards of the boardwalk below. A splintering crash of wood rent the silence and there was a muffled cry. An instant later the fallen man was struggling to push away the débris of the awning that covered him.

Clee came to his feet, his Colt swinging around to cover the man who had come so near to killing him. The oldster rose sheepishly, his rifle forgotten, one hand gingerly rubbing a bruised thigh.

He growled a curse, and called out: "I aimed to kill you, stranger!"

Clee's words carried sharply across the short space that separated them: "I reckon I know that by now. But why?"

He didn't get a reply from the oldster. A crowd was gathering, and out from the walk stepped a spare-framed man wearing a five-pointed sheriff's star on his shirt front. He stopped five paces short of Clee and said flatly: "You might save yourself some trouble by ridin' straight on through, King. We can settle things here our own way. Put up that smoke-pole."

Clee slowly dropped his Colt back into its holster, then said shortly: "My handle isn't King, and you can settle your troubles any way you like. Why did that ranny try a bushwhack?"

The sheriff shook his head stubbornly. It was a crisp fall day, yet beads of perspiration stood out on his forehead. "We don't bluff, Gunnar. If you buy into any more gun play here, there's enough of us comin' after you so that your iron won't take care of us all. Ben, here, is a friend of Steve Hall's. He was drunk, or he wouldn't have made a try at you. But there's no use hidin' who you are. You're ridin' a palomino and there's the way you wear your cutter. That's enough for us."

Clee frowned, yet kept his patience. It was plain that he had been mistaken for someone else, so he answered: "Which will it be, Sheriff? First, you call me King, now it's Gunnar."

"You're Gunnar King and we've been expectin' you. Do like I said and ride away. We don't need the help of any owlhoot outsiders in settlin' this."

"Have it your way." Clee shrugged, seeing that the crowd behind the sheriff was regarding him stonily. Then he had a sudden thought and added: "Tell me where I can find this Steve Hall."

The sheriff's brown eyes widened a shade: "Hall?" He shook his head. "You let Steve and his girl alone, King, unless you want trouble. Miles Banning is the man who brought you in. See him if you see anybody."

Clee Adams planted his hands on his hips and spread his feet a little, confronting the lawman squarely: "Either you're loco or I am, tin star. My handle is Gunnar King, you say. And I can't see

175

Steve Hall, but should see this gent Banning first. Is this Wagon Fork, or do you want to make it Kansas City? What'll it be?"

The lawman's eyes were blazing now, although a measure of fear tinged his glance. "I've had my say, King. You've been warned, which is all that's necessary." Keeping his eyes on Clee's hands, he backed across the street to the walk, where he stood, backed by the group that surrounded the oldster and the broken awning.

There was no softness in the glances of the crowd over there, no sign of tolerance that would have let Clee show them the mistake they were making. His palomino wore no brand, a thing that would be hard to explain. So he turned and picked up the stallion's trailing reins and led him to the opposite hitch rail.

Several doors beyond was the sign reading **Tyler House**. Tying the palomino, he stepped up to the walk and started for the hotel, thinking to see Steve Hall and learn the reasons for what had happened. Across the way the crowd was breaking up.

"King."

That name, spoken softly beside him, made Clee turn quickly to search out the speaker. Before the batwing doors of the Catamount Saloon stood a man with the trace of a shrewd smile on his square-jawed face. He was outfitted expensively in a clean white shirt and string tie, and gray whipcord trousers stuffed into the fancy-stitched boots. He wore two pearl-handled guns low-slung in tooled holsters.

"Come in and we'll have a talk, King," he said. "I'm Miles Banning. This is my place."

Clee's temper was wearing thin. He cuffed his Stetson back on his head and said sharply: "The next jasper who calls me by that handle buys himself some trouble. You got that straight, stranger?"

The man in the doorway held up a protesting hand. "Don't be proddy, King. We all know who you are." He dropped his hand and his look took on a less compromising quality. "What's all this talk you were givin' the sheriff about seein' Steve Hall?"

"That's what I'm here for."

Miles Banning nodded, and his black eyes lighted with a momentary cunning. Then, with a jerk of his head, he signaled someone inside. Instantly there stepped through the doors a tall, lean man with inscrutable pale blue eyes. He had a pair of Colt .45s lined at Clee.

"Think again, King," Banning said. "I say you're comin' inside."

Clee let his hands fall to his sides in a deliberately stubborn gesture. It brought a look of alarm to Miles Banning's face. "Don't draw!" the saloon owner said hastily. "I've heard of you drawin' against a man with his guns on you, only don't try it now!" He turned to the man alongside him. "Put your irons away, Sam." He sighed with relief as Sam's guns dropped back into leather, then said with a note of pleading in his voice: "We can use each other, King. Hear what I have to say before you see Steve Hall."

Some instinct told Clee that here was the thing he wanted. He knew nothing of Steve Hall and the things that were involved here. Why not listen to what Banning had to say and get the whole story before he saw this Steve Hall? So he lifted his broad shoulders in a shrug and drawled: "There's plenty of time for my business with Hall. I'll come in."

II

It was late afternoon, and the Catamount was crowded. As Banning led Clee inside, a hush settled over the big room and all eyes turned to watch the entrance of this stranger with a mixture of awe and respect. Clee felt the tension without looking. He had been saddled with the name of an outlaw, one whose guns evidently carried a potent and respected threat. That would explain the attitude of this crowd, which already knew what had happened on the street three minutes ago.

Banning led the way to the rear and started up a flight of stairs to the balcony that ran around three sides of the room. Looking up there, Clee could see eight or ten doors opening off the balcony, probably rooms used by the percentage girls he saw elbowing the bar or sitting with the men at the tables.

Sam, the man who had held the guns on him out front, stopped at the foot of the stairway and stepped aside for him to pass. But Clee smiled thinly and said: "You first, brother."

Sam grinned, and went on ahead, but Clee caught in the man's eyes a hint of the disappointment he felt at the failure of his ruse. Clee was both amused and wary as he followed Sam, for Miles Banning couldn't be trusted far with men like this carrying out his orders.

Banning entered a room, and Clee, coming abreast the doorway, looked inside to see the saloon owner taking a chair behind an ornate cherry-wood desk at the back wall. He followed Sam closely and was stepping through the door when his sideward glance caught sight of three men who stood half hidden along the left-hand wall.

Sensing the reasons for the presence of these three, Clee reached out and planted his fist in the back of Sam's shirt and jerked the man toward him as a shield. At the same time his right hand flashed to the butt of his Colt. He rocked the gun out with blurring speed, lined it at the three along the side wall, and then shoved Sam out of the way into the room.

He had caught them utterly by surprise, their hands closed on the handles of their guns. They were all of the same breed, hard-eyed, sober-faced, wicked-looking, killers to a man. And now, recognizing the only threat that could possibly have influenced them, they slowly raised their hands from their weapons.

"Reception committee?" Clee drawled, glancing at Miles Banning.

The saloon owner's face went red. He forced a smile, turned a glance of contempt on his three gunmen, then looked back at Clee and said: "That was smooth, Gunnar, as smooth a play as I've seen in a long time. I can use you."

Clee was looking at the others. "Shell out the hardware, gents," he drawled, and stood waiting until they had gingerly lifted their weapons from holsters and dropped them to the faded carpet, Sam along with the others. Then Clee crossed the room and sat on the corner of Banning's desk. "Talk fast, Banning," he said curtly. "No one often treats me this way."

Banning's two hands opened and closed nervously. He reached out and opened a box of cigars on the desk top and offered them to Clee, who refused. Banning took one, bit off the end, and ran his hands over his shirt pockets for a match. Finding none, he casually dipped into the top drawer of the desk. Instantly Clee leaned over and clamped a hand on the man's wrist, then reached into the drawer himself and lifted out the gun lying there. He tossed it to the carpet along with the others and said: "Maybe you ought to hand over your irons too, Banning."

Then, after Banning had sullenly lifted out the two guns in his holsters and put them on the desk, Clee reached into his pocket and gave Banning a match before he picked up the weapons and rammed them into his belt.

"You've got me wrong, King," Banning protested. "I'm quite willing to . . ."

"Talk," Clee put in. "Tell me the whole thing from the beginning."

"You know what my letter said. That's about all there is . . ."

"My memory's not so good. Better say the whole thing over again so I can get it straight. Remember, Banning, I haven't said I'd hire out to you. There's this Steve Hall to think of."

Banning's look became hard and his black eyes lighted with an inner fire. "Steve Hall. He can't pay you enough to make it worth your time. I saw to that."

Clee raised his brows quizzically. "Go ahead."

Banning leaned across the desk, regarding Clee with a narrow-lidded gaze. "It's like my letter said. Hall has bought into something that isn't his business. A year ago I loaned this man Art Mason five thousand on his outfit, the Box M. Art was broke and couldn't get the money at the bank.

Then he took down sick. That was last winter, and I could see I'd have to foreclose on him to get my money back. His herds are mighty thin, and the place never did pay."

"Art Mason?" Clee repeated the unfamiliar name. "Then how come you loaned him the money?"

Banning smiled cunningly. "I'd looked into the thing and had my men go over this range, every inch of it. They found something." He paused to let his words have their effect on Clee. When he got no comment, he went on: "They found placer gold in Dry Bone Creek, high up in the hills on Mason's range. That's why I let him have the money."

"And Steve Hall?" Clee queried.

Banning's face twisted into an ugly mask. "Hall was the gent that sold Art Mason that land in the first place. Art was his friend before he came here. So when I threatened to foreclose, Steve set up a howl you could have heard clear to the border. He's given Mason the money to meet his interest payments on the note, but I'm foreclosin' anyway."

"Did Hall find out why you wanted the layout?"

"He did." Banning nodded. "I'll give that *hombre* credit. He found where we'd sunk a test pit up above Dry Bone, and guessed what it was. He went to the bank, borrowed five thousand, and was goin' to pay off Mason's mortgage and send Mason to a hospital in Denver. But someone busted into Hall's safe the other night after he got that money. Now he hasn't got it and the bank's just reorganized and isn't in shape to give him any more. Mason's busted, I got Steve Hall where I want him, and now we'll finish the job. Mason's note is due the twenty-eighth, three days from now. He won't be able to pay."

"It couldn't have been your men who took the money, could it?"

Banning's smile broadened, but he made no answer. That seemed to satisfy Clee for he drawled: "So then you sent for me. Why?"

"Hall will fight," Banning explained. "He's got a salty outfit. He's also got the law behind him. If they had proof of a few things, I'd be in jail. But they haven't, and, after I've finished with Mason and Hall, I'm going to whip this town into shape and call it mine, sheriff and all."

"So you want me to go after him?" Clee queried. His mind was occupied with the vision he had had of Steve's Hall's daughter on the trail into town, and he was wondering, too, what Hall would be like.

Banning's eyes became slitted and he looked up at Clee with a shrewdness creeping into his glance. "Maybe I've told you too much. You asked for Hall when you drifted into town. Maybe it's your turn to talk."

Without hesitation Clee varied the lie that had

183

Schmaling Mem. Pub. Library
501 Tenth Avenue
Fulton, IL 61252

been in his mind for minutes now. "Hall said he'd pay me good money to come in on his side. I always aim to back the law whenever I can."

Banning chuckled, then laughed outright, leaning back in his chair, his whole frame shaking with mirth. Finally he sobered enough to say: "That's a good one, King! You on the side of the law." His joviality faded, and he turned suddenly serious. "I'll pay you double what Steve Hall offered."

Clee shrugged his shoulders and got up off the edge of the desk and reached into his shirt pocket for tobacco and papers. As his long fingers fashioned a cigarette, he said: "Send these fake hardcases of yours out of here, Banning. I'll make my deal with you alone."

Banning looked across at his men. "Wait down below, boys," he said. "Sam, you stay."

"Sam can go, too," Clee said, without looking up from his hands. "And let those guns stay where they are."

He didn't see Banning's shrewd look fasten on Sam, nor catch Sam's helpless gesture. Only after the door was closed behind Banning's four men did Clee look up. Then he crossed to the door, turned the key in the lock, and took a chair against the side wall so that he could watch Banning and the window above his head and the door.

He scratched a match and held the flame to the cigarette, drawing in the smoke in a gusty breath.

Then, abruptly, he said: "I'll do your job for five thousand."

The saloon owner's thick frame lunged up out of the chair. Fists on the desk top, face flushed, he leaned forward and fastened his granite-like glance on Clee. "I'd figured you'd swing it for five hundred," he said silkily. "It's only a couple days' work."

"Dry-gulchin' comes high these days, Banning. Take it or leave it. If you don't hire me, Hall will. Then it'll be you that stops one of my slugs. That's a promise."

Sweat poured out on Miles Banning's brow. He sat down in his chair slowly, a heavy weariness seeming to sap his strength. Clee pressed his point. "You can give me the five thousand you took from Hall. It's worth it. You're gettin' a gold mine, aren't you? With me against you, you'll never get a clear title to Mason's layout, and maybe you won't even live long enough to see who gets it."

That outright threat brought a trace of fear to Banning's countenance. Clee was wondering if the name of Gunnar King could carry enough weight to back so open a threat. It did, for Banning straightened in his chair with a mirthless smile.

"It's a deal," he muttered. "Only see that you shoot square with me, Gunnar. No runnin' to Steve Hall."

"That's another thing," Clee interrupted. "I'm going to see Hall."

Banning's features set inscrutably. "At least you're honest," he began. "You're savin' me . . ."

"I'm savin' you nothing. I'm going to Hall and pretend to hire out to him. In that way we'll know what kind of a fight he's buildin'. When the right time comes, I'll let you know and we can frame the whole works."

Banning's features lost their grimness, and a look of sheer disbelief took possession of them. "You'd . . . you'd do that?" His blunt fist crashed down on the desk. "It'll work, King. We can get Hall any time we want him."

Clee stood up and stretched lazily. "I'll take the money now. Five thousand."

"Wait until morning," Banning suggested. "The bank's closed now and . . ."

Clee nodded toward the safe behind Banning's desk. That nod was the same as a spoken word, stopping Banning in mid-sentence. He surveyed this tall, lean stranger and evidently made the immediate decision that no amount of bluffing could carry his point.

He nodded. "You're plenty slick, Gunnar," he said, and turned to the safe and began spinning the dial.

Clee stood close behind Banning as the door to the safe swung open. He saw a blunt-nosed .45 lying ready in the biggest compartment, and watched Banning's hand closely. But the saloon owner pointedly avoided touching the gun and lifted out a tin box that he put on his desk. He opened it, took out a sheaf of bills, and counted out a stack, putting the box back in the safe when he had finished.

He pushed the bills across to the far side of the desk, toward Clee, and said: "There it is, count it."

Clee picked up the banknotes, folded them into two equal bundles, and put them in the pockets of his Levi's. "I'll take your word for it, Banning. You wouldn't run a sandy on me now."

Banning queried: "What'll the play be from now on? I want this done fast, but so they won't be able to hang it on me or any of my men. That's why I sent for you."

"I hear Hall's in town," Clee said. "I'll try to hire out to him. Maybe I'll ride out to his layout if I can't find him. You'll hear from me in a day or two. I'll come here if I have anything for you."

Steve Hall would be at the hotel waiting for Matt Byne's messenger. That much Clee knew. He didn't go to the hotel, but instead sauntered down the street to his rail-haltered palomino. The main thoroughfare of Wagon Fork was deep in shadow now, for the sun had dipped over the far rim of the hills to the west and only high above, on the far peaks of the Iron Claws fifty miles to the east, was the light of day still strong.

He swung up into the saddle again, not knowing how to get to Art Mason's place but assuming that it lay west of town, toward the hills, for Banning had mentioned Dry Bone Creek as being in the hills, and they lay close in only one direction. As he left town, he felt the glances of the curious upon him, and what little expression he could catch on people's faces in the fading light showed him the same grim looks that had greeted him as he entered town. Steve Hall and Art Mason obviously had the support of the towns-people, and his stamping himself as Banning's man on his visit to the Catamount had only deepened that feeling of antagonism they felt toward him.

The name of Banning isn't popular around here, he told himself, looking at the thing honestly. From all Banning had told him of Hall and Mason, they were in the right and honest to the core. For the first time in his life, Clee Adams felt a doubt as to his attitude toward men like Steve Hall, a rancher who ran a big outfit, the kind of man he had schooled himself to hate. Steve Hall was fighting to save a friend, spending his own money to see that Art Mason got what was rightfully his, and this fact somehow clashed with all Clee's stubborn, hate-born theories.

Angrily he brushed aside this thought that conflicted with his own way of thinking. In order to rid his mind completely of the doubt that was growing there, he tried to think of his own good fortune in having seen Miles Banning before he saw Steve Hall. Banning had steered him to a real find, for he had $10,000 now, and with that money he'd buy into Art Mason's layout in some way and build up a fortune within a few years. His time-tempered hatred for Matt Byne was still strong, and it was easy to convince himself that Steve Hall was probably the same kind of man. He would have to fight Banning in this, but he had been bred with a gun in his hand and with a fearlessness that now made him laugh at the thought of what the saloon owner would do when he discovered this betrayal. He was betraying Hall and Matt Byne, too, but that was as it should be.

Two miles beyond town he heard a low rumble coming up out of the half darkness behind. He pulled off the trail and reined in to listen. Soon he identified the sound as the ring of iron-tired wheels on the solidly packed trail, and, with the assurance that whoever was coming was not bringing danger to him, he went on again at a slow trot.

In five minutes he turned in the saddle and made out a buckboard pulled by a team of fast-trotting blacks. He reined to the side again and waited for it to pass. It was almost abreast of him when he discerned through the half light the girl he had seen that afternoon on the trail the other side of town. As the buckboard drew alongside, the girl's look measured him and recognition came. She said something to the man beside her, and his arms tightened on the reins, and he pulled the team to an abrupt stop.

It was the man, old and grizzled, who took Clee's attention then. Even in this light he could catch the angry look that flashed in Steve Hall's eyes—for this must be Hall riding with his daughter.

"So you're Gunnar King," Hall said dryly. Then, suddenly straightening where he sat, he muttered: "And you're here to back Banning's forked play."

"That's a funny thing," Clee drawled, "you callin' me King along with the rest. You're all wrong. Clee Adams is my rightful name, and I came here lookin' for a place to invest a little money in grass and critters."

"I'm Steve Hall," came the flat announcement. "I wondered what kind of a lame excuse you'd give me. Now's the time to make your try." And with those words Hall's hands stabbed down at the six-gun in the waistband of his Levi's. He yanked it out and swiveled it up at Clee, who sat his saddle, unmoving.

"Maybe you'd like proof," Clee said, his stomach tightening at sight of the fierce blazing of the rancher's eyes. Then, slowly, so that his move would not be misread, he reached into a back pocket and brought out a worn leather wallet. Inside it he found a slip of yellowed paper. He unfolded it and handed it across to Hall, who took it without once taking his eyes from Clee's.

"You see what this says, Sis," the rancher said to the girl, handing her the paper, his gun held rock steady.

Betty Hall examined it closely, barely able to make out the printing in the fading light. Suddenly she straightened, gave a quick gasp, and said: "Dad, he's right! His name is Clee Adams. Here's a cattle registration made out in his name, signed by a Colorado sheriff."

Reluctantly Hall laid down his weapon and took the paper. After looking at it, he raised his eyes and regarded Clee soberly. Then he said: "I reckon I made a mistake." He sighed wearily, and ran his hand over his brow. "This thing's got me whipped. No word from Matt today, Mason down in bed again, and Banning ready to close out on us and steal everything Art has to his name."

"Banning made me a proposition an hour ago," Clee said. "He still thinks I'm King. By rights, you should know what he had to say. Isn't there some place where we could sit down and talk this over? I came here to invest some money, like I told you, in good grass and a few feeders. But from what Banning tells me I can use what I have to better advantage by makin' this Art Mason a loan. How would that sound to you?"

"Are you tellin' this straight from the shoulder?" Hall said incredulously, a new hope showing in his shadowed glance. That look made Clee uncomfortable and he was thankful for the fading light that hid his embarrassment.

"It's gospel," he insisted. "I'm on my way to Mason's place now."

Steve Hall was convinced, a conviction that showed now in the warmth that crept back into his expression. "We've got three more miles to ride. Sis can cook us a supper and we'll give Art something to think about. Let's get goin'." He slapped his blacks with the reins, and the vehicle lurched forward, Clee falling in alongside.

The girl glanced sideways at Clee several times with an appraising expression that increased his discomfort. Once he intercepted her glance and caught her confused smile. It was too dark to see, but he imagined that her color deepened as she looked away again. To think that this girl believed in him was going to make it hard.

III

There were two reasons why no one saw the stranger ride into Wagon Fork. The first was that he entered town during the supper hour, when most men who would have been interested in seeing him were eating; the second, that he made a quarter circle of the town in the darkness and rode directly to the livery stable corral, passing no house on his way in from open country. He turned his palomino into the pole enclosure after having loosened the cinch, and then made his way through to the street by taking the passageway between the two nearest buildings.

He was of medium build, with sloping shoulders and thickly muscled arms. His eyes were slate-colored, bleak, and he wore only one glove, on his left hand. His single Colt .38 rode high at his left thigh, butt foremost, in the manner Clee Adams had worn his.

When the awninged walk led him past the lighted store windows, this stranger pulled his broad-brimmed Stetson low over his eyes and made directly for the Catamount. Inside the saloon he stepped to the bar and asked the bartender: "Where's the boss?"

There was a brittle quality in his voice that made the apron man examine him with more than casual interest, although the examination ended quickly for the stranger's look invited no prolonged inspection. The bartender said: "He's up in his office, third door beyond the stairs on the balcony."

The stranger walked straight to the stairs, climbed them, and, when he had counted three doors, he unhesitatingly twisted the knob of the third and entered.

Miles Banning's feet were on the desk, a cigar was clenched between his teeth, and he was speaking to Sam. He broke off abruptly to see who it was that entered his office without knocking. His look sharpened in critical inspection of this stranger, yet the protest that rose within him was never voiced. He saw in the stranger the same quality that had made the bartender below give his respectful answer.

Instead of the wrathful explosion another man's unannounced entrance would have prompted, Banning asked levelly: "Well?"

The stranger shot a look at Sam, then let his eyes settle on Banning once more. "I'll make my talk with you alone, Banning."

The saloon owner hesitated in his answer only long enough to get his feet down off the desk. Then, having made his decision quickly, he said, while still measuring the stranger: "Wait for me down below, Sam."

As the door closed behind Sam, the stranger stepped to an inside corner of the room and for the first time allowed some of the hardness to leave his countenance. "I'm here, Banning," he announced. "What's the play?"

For two long seconds Banning's expression was one of bafflement, then, quickly enough, he picked out the one point that could give him a clue to this man's identity—the butt-fronted gun in the holster at the stranger's left thigh. Banning's eyes narrowed as he drawled: "You can't be Gunnar King?"

The stranger nodded his answer and held his silence.

Banning cursed softly, a trace of helplessness in his glance. Finally he asked: "How am I to know for sure?"

Gunnar King's left hand dipped into his shirt pocket and brought out a crumpled piece of paper. He tossed it on the desk, and Banning picked it up. He unfolded it and breathed: "My letter!"

"What's the play?" the outlaw asked tonelessly, for the second time.

"It's changed some since I wrote this," was Banning's unsteady answer. "We've got another little job on our hands. Yes, sir, another job. This afternoon a gent wearing a plow handle for a cross draw rode in here on a palomino. Someone tacked your handle onto him, and before he left town he had five thousand of my money. It was pay for the thing I brought you in for."

King whistled softly, then chuckled in obvious mirth. "You don't look that easy, Banning."

The saloon owner's lips were set in a thin tight line. "He took me in like a greenhorn. We'll have to move fast."

Gunnar King's brows raised in question: "We? What do you aim to do about it, friend? A man smart enough to take that much money off you would be smart enough to head straight for the hills. Maybe you ought to tell me about it."

But Banning showed no inclination to elaborate on what had happened. He got up from his chair, crossed to the door, and, swinging it open, bawled out: "Sam! Round up the boys and get ready to ride." Then, seeming to remember King, he turned and said curtly: "I'll tell you about it on the way out. We're goin' to take a sashay out along the west trail, to Art Mason's place."

It wasn't until after supper that they gathered around Art Mason's bed for serious talk. Betty Hall had prepared the meal and the four of them had eaten it in comparative silence, Steve Hall purposely avoiding any mention to Mason of his reason for bringing Clee on this visit.

Now, for the first time, Clee had the chance to study Mason. The man lay in a clean-sheeted bed, his wasted frame propped up on a mound of pillows, his gaunt face seamed with lines of pain, and his eyes bright with a fever that heightened the color of the tight skin over his cheek bones. Clee had seen this before, a sick man whose lungs had gone bad on him, but never had he seen one whose fate he could read so clearly. Art Mason's days were already numbered.

He felt a grudging admiration for these three— for the man who so stubbornly clung to life, for Steve Hall, who was sticking by a friend, and for

the girl. Clee also was impressed by the serious-
ness that pervaded Mason's place. Outside, Hall's
riders rode guard around the pastures—they had
been challenged by them coming in along the
trail—and a half dozen men were within call in
the yard out back, men who carried rifles and
wore six-guns belted about their waists.
Banning's claim that Steve Hall ran a salty outfit
was no idle statement.

Hall turned up the lamp so that its light fell
fully on Clee's face, and said: "Art, it looks like
we're in luck. Adams, here, tells a queer story but
one that listens straight. He rode into town today
thinkin' to look over the country and maybe
make an investment in cattle and land. He rode a
palomino, and you can see how he wears his
cutter. It was natural that someone took him for
Gunnar King and started talkin'. The story got
around and Banning heard it. You can fill in the
rest, Adams."

The girl leaned forward in her chair, studying
Clee intently, and Art Mason elbowed up off his
pillows, all attention.

"It's like Hall says," Clee began, speaking to
Mason. "Banning and the rest tagged me with
this King's name. Who is King?"

"An outlaw. Poison!" Mason growled. "For the
last five years he's been houndin' the towns north
o' here, within reach of his hide-out up in the hills.
There was talk a while ago of Banning bringin'

197

him in to go against us. We thought it was nothin' but talk, but it don't look that way now."

Clee took this in, then said: "First off, an old codger tried to put a bullet into me. Then the sheriff asked me to ride on through. I was headed for the hotel when Banning stopped me and said he'd like to have a talk. I went into his place. He wouldn't listen when I gave him my real name, but said I was King and that he'd hired me to come in and do a job for him. I let him talk. He told me about your mortgage, Mason, and said that he'd found gold on your place and was goin' to take it. I fed him more rope and he owned up to robbin' Hall's safe the other night."

Steve Hall straightened in his chair and said hotly: "I reckon that sort of proof will carry with the sheriff. Now we've got Miles Banning where we want him."

"He's out to get you," Clee went on. "In fact, he offered me money to hire out to bushwhack you. I smelled a skunk and told him he'd have to show me hard cash. He did. I named a big figure, five thousand, and held out for it, hopin' to scare him off. But he paid me. Here's the money."

He reached inside his shirt, opened two of the pockets of his money belt, and pulled out two tight rolls of paper money. Putting them on the table in front of Hall, he said: "I reckon this money is yours, since it's what Banning took out of your safe."

The rancher's face had blanched a shade at hearing this evidence against Banning, but now he reached for the money and picked it up with a hand that trembled.

"You'd better count it," Clee suggested. "I took Banning's word that it was all there."

Hall smoothed out the money and started fingering through it. But his hand was unsteady and finally, in desperation, he handed it to his daughter, saying gruffly: "You count it, Sis."

The girl took the money and laid it in her lap and started leafing through it. At that moment Clee remembered that part of the money she was counting was Matt Byne's, for in his haste at the saloon he had opened a pocket of his belt that contained half of what he had found in Matt's gun. The hint of a smile drew out the line of his thin lips as he remembered that part of his plan had been to use Matt Byne's money as his own, and he watched the girl as she went about her task.

Then Art Mason interrupted his thoughts by saying: "It's mighty square of you to do this, Adams. My note to Banning is due in three days. I didn't think I'd ever pay it off, but now I can. We owe you a lot."

Clee's smile broadened, but he shook his head. "You don't owe me a thing. But I have a few thousand more of my own I'd like to throw in with this to see you through your trouble. If you're wantin' to do me a favor, sell me an interest in your place. You can have my money, my gun, and what little I know of workin' a mine. I'm bein' selfish in a way, since it looks as though I'd make money out of it along with the rest of you."

It was because he was so intent on Art Mason's answer that he failed to see the girl pull the white slip of paper from out of the bundle of money in her lap. Her father missed it, too, because he was too absorbed in listening to what Clee was saying.

In the five-second silence that followed Clee's words, Betty Hall's eyes scanned the lines of the message Matt Byne had sent along with the money. Her head jerked up and for a moment her brown eyes flashed with the bright light of anger as she regarded Clee. Then that expression changed to one of puzzlement, and she abruptly crumpled the paper and tucked it up the sleeve of her blouse as her father spoke.

Steve Hall said: "I reckon any help you'd give us right now would entitle you to a share, Adams. After all, there was no reason why you had to turn this money over to us. Not many men would have done that." The rancher glanced at Art Mason and asked: "Is that your way of thinkin', Art?"

Art Mason nodded emphatically. "I'm owin' both of you more than I'll ever be able to pay back. Let's make a three-way split on whatever comes out of that gold pocket, Steve."

Hall shook his head. "I've told you before that

I'm not takin' any part of what's rightfully yours, Art. I'm loanin' you this money. Pay it back when you have it."

Mason smiled mysteriously, and murmured: "You're stubborn as the devil, Steve. But someday I'll have my say in all this. You mark my words."

Steve Hall seemed to catch something of significance in Mason's statement. Knowing that his friend foresaw what would soon happen to him, the rancher said gruffly: "You're talkin' like a fool, Art!" He rose up out of his chair and added hastily: "We'll be goin' now. I'm takin' Adams over to my place for the night. Tomorrow we can settle all this and I'll take the money into town and pay off Banning's note for you. And I'm leavin' word with Hogan and the rest to pack your things and get you ready for tomorrow afternoon's stage, Art. You're goin' to that hospital in Denver and get well."

Mason protested, but Steve Hall and his daughter pressed the point and the invalid finally consented. It was arranged that Hogan, Hall's foreman on duty outside, should bring Art Mason into Wagon Fork in a buckboard the following day, and that Mason would leave for Denver and let Hall and Clee take care of his affairs in his absence.

As they were leaving, Mason proffered his hand to Clee and tried his best to match Clee's firm grasp. "Thanks," was all the man could manage to say, but that one word was so expressive of his deep gratitude that it brought up a self-loathing within Clee he could not put down during the long ride west to Steve Hall's ranch.

For the second time that night, Clee questioned his motives. Steve Hall and his daughter—and Art Mason, for that matter—seemed like the real sort. But once more a stubbornness fed through the past year asserted itself. *This is your chance, take it* was his thought as he rode alongside the buckboard.

Steve Hall's layout had a prosperous look. There were seven outbuildings nestled around the spacious adobe house, which was sprawled in a grove of cottonwoods beside a stream. The place was deserted, for the crew was riding guard on Mason's place.

Steve Hall was obviously worn out from a day in which disappointment had sapped his strength. He got down stiffly from the buckboard as he pulled the team to a stop in the yard, and Clee, seeing the weariness that had taken hold of the man, offered: "Let me take the team down and unhitch. You turn in."

Hall gave him a grateful look. "You show him where to hang up the harness, will you, Sis? I think I'll take you up on it, Adams. See you in the morning."

At the barn Clee busied himself with unhitching the team and carrying the harness into the wagon shed. The girl stood by, her tallness accentuated by the light of a lantern on the ground behind her.

Twice Clee caught her coolly appraising him. It had been the same earlier that night, only now her glance didn't waver when it met his.

Finally she asked: "What made you offer us your help? There's really nothing we can show you to prove that you'll get your money out of this."

"I'm a gambler. I usually win."

"Did you make your money gambling?" she asked with a strange intensity of tone that made him look at her more closely.

"You might call it that."

She was silent a moment, watching him work. Then: "Miles Banning is a gambler, too. Years ago, down in Texas, he gambled and lost. He was trusted with money, and he took it and left that part of the state and took a new name and set himself up in business. Somehow, people learned what he'd done. He moved and tried to make another start. That happened four times. The thing's followed him up here and made him what he is . . . hated by every decent man. Once he might have been decent and had the right qualities for being a fine man. But the thing he did warped his nature, until now he's too low to crawl. He's the only gambler I know."

Clee, listening to a story the beginning of which so closely paralleled his own beginning, was held wordless for many seconds. Finally he forced a laugh and said: "All gamblers don't turn out that way. Besides, I'm not a professional gambler like Banning."

"I hope not." Then, looking at him dispassionately, she added: "No, you couldn't be. I'm sure that however you got your start, it was honest."

She held out her hand and he took it, feeling that her grasp was firm and warm. "Good night, Mister Adams. We're glad you're to be our friend. It isn't often Dad trusts a man at first sight. But he's trusting you . . . and so am I."

Her face flushed suddenly as she realized that he still held her hand. She gently released her grasp and turned and went on up to the house. She went through to the kitchen and found Louie, the Chinese cook, sitting on his high stool before the big wood range. Louie always made it a point to be the last to turn in. As she came to the door, he got down off his stool and reached for the coffee pot.

"Will it keep me awake, Louie?" she asked.

He shook his head and grinned broadly. "Louie's coffee put you to sleep."

She sipped her coffee, finding it strangely bitter to the taste.

"Louie," she said abruptly, "what would you think if someone you knew, someone you thought you could like, wasn't what he seemed?" As soon as she had put the question, she realized its absurdity.

Louie's look was momentarily puzzled. Then he yawned and stretched. "Louie go to bed and sleep on it," he murmured, and with that he shuffled across his kitchen and disappeared through the outside door.

His answer, which was no answer at all, made her laugh, for to apply his words was probably the only advice anyone could have given her. As she went to her room, she once more told herself that she would confide in no one, not even her father, until she had given Clee Adams enough rope to hang himself.

IV

Afterward, Clee took the lantern, went to the bunkhouse, undressed, and turned in. He tossed restlessly in the unfamiliar bunk. At first it was the bulk of the money belt around his waist that made him uncomfortable. He got up and took it off, but even then sleep wouldn't come to ease the ache of his trail-weary muscles. He sat up in the bunk, rolled a cigarette, and watched the pinpoint glow of its ash in the blackness, thinking of Betty Hall.

What she had said had touched him with surprising directness, and for a moment he was panic-stricken by the thought that somehow she had discovered what he was doing. But then he told himself that it wasn't possible. How could she know? No, that wasn't the answer. Some strange insight had framed her words and made her speak of Banning, and his warped life. He shuddered involuntarily as he reviewed the picture she had painted—the picture that made him put himself in Banning's place. Years from now he might be a second Miles Banning.

"You're dreamin', Adams!"

He laughed aloud, but his own voice echoed in the empty room to mock him. He wouldn't have taken that story seriously, coming from any other person. But he had found something in the girl that he was starving for—a glimpse of beauty, of a gentleness he could never possess, and he suddenly realized that three hours with Betty Hall had made him feel more deeply toward her than he had ever felt toward a woman. And suddenly he believed in the things she had pointed out, believed that Banning's ultimate failure was hinged on that first dishonest act. At that moment, sitting alone in the darkness of an unfamiliar bunkhouse, Clee Adams threw off the hatreds and misdeeds of his past and realized that he had headed far down the wrong trail. Matt Byne had probably been right in what he did. He'd paid a good price to the squatters for their beef and in the bargain had offered them jobs at a time when jobs were scarce.

For a moment his pride made him almost hate

206

Betty Hall for having so unknowingly pointed out his weakness. But then that spark of hatred died before a finer feeling, a feeling that he recognized as the beginning of something he had never before experienced. As surely as he felt it, just as surely did he know that he had made it impossible to have this girl's respect. He had stolen Matt Byne's money and bought himself in too solidly with these people ever to make good the harm he had done.

What was he to do to make it up to these three —to save Art Mason's ranch and to keep Miles Banning from carrying out his plans? He was one man against a dozen of Banning's hardcases. He could manage the rest, all but Banning. It gave him a grim satisfaction to realize the change that had come over him. None of the things along his back trail, none of the hatreds of these last four years, counted now. He, Clee Adams, whose gun had always fought the range hogs, was now siding with a man he would have hated a week ago, or even a day ago.

Strangely enough, once the decision had taken root in his mind, it wiped away all the tension that had been there during the past few hours. Instead of trying to sleep, he now fought a drowsiness that crept through him. He tried to stay awake and think of Betty Hall, for he was wondering what it was about him she suspected, how much she knew. But sleep finally overtook him.

He was awake at sunup, and his first thought centered on Miles Banning. Today he'd see Banning. What would happen he couldn't guess, but, when he was through with Banning, Art Mason's troubles would be over.

He was on his way to the kitchen when one of Hall's riders streaked into the yard and around to the front of the house. The cowpuncher brought news of a raid at Mason's place the night before, a raid that had been met by the guns of Hall's riders. It hadn't lasted long, for the night riders had been surprised in finding the ranch guarded and had wasted no time in riding away in the darkness.

Steve Hall, hearing the cowpuncher's story, was emphatic. "It was Banning," he said to Clee, his tone one of puzzlement. "Now what would make that jasper jump the gun that way? For all he knows he'll have a clear title to Art's place inside the next three days."

Clee couldn't explain Banning's move, and soon gave up trying to discover the reason for the raid. What he had to say to Steve Hall was more important. After breakfast, when he and the rancher were alone, Hall gave him an opening.

"I've been thinkin' the thing over, Adams," Hall said. "With this five thousand you've turned over to us, I can pay off Art's note to Banning today, but unless we have more money to go on, it may be years before we can start workin' that vein.

Would you take half interest in Mason's place for the other money you say you want to throw into the thing?"

Clee nodded. "But what about your share?"

Hall shrugged his shoulders in faint irritation. "Art's loco when he talks about swingin' me in on this. He doesn't owe me a thing for what I've done, and I won't have it. With this place on its feet in another year or two I'll have all any man could want. The bank and the weather have caught me a little short right now, but that can't last. You and Art go at this thing together, half and half, and get what you can out of it."

"A partnership is a bigger slice than I deserve."

"It's not," insisted Hall. "Mason couldn't have gone ahead but for you. I want to see the thing get under way, to give Art something to take his mind off his lungs."

"It's good enough for me," Clee agreed after a moment's hesitation. "We'll meet Mason in town before he leaves this afternoon and have a deed drawn up. Another thing. I'd like to take this money in to Banning myself. Will you let me handle it alone?"

"You mean you'd walk in to Banning alone . . . with all the hardcases he can throw against you?"

Clee nodded.

Steve Hall's weathered visage looked grim, and his eyes lighted for an instant with a distinct distrust. "I take it you've got your reasons for askin' this. What are they?"

"Banning's put a bounty on you, Hall, but I can walk into this office and see him alone, without his knowin' what's comin'. Remember, he still thinks I'm in with him, that I'm Gunnar King. Once I'm there, I'll get Art Mason's canceled note some way. And another thing. Let's keep this to ourselves. Don't even tell your daughter what we're doin'. I wouldn't want her to worry about it."

The rancher's reaction was as Clee expected, for a grateful smile came to Steve Hall's countenance and he seemed entirely reassured. "You're the right kind of a pardner, Adams. Work this any way you think best. I'll be backin' you all the way."

They met Art Mason in town at three that afternoon. The first thing they did was to see Holcomb, Steve Hall's lawyer, who drew up a new deed to Mason's ranch, naming Clee as half owner. Mason at first insisted that Steve Hall was to come in on the partnership, but the rancher stubbornly refused. Finally Mason gave in before Hall's argument, and the deed was signed and notarized, naming Clee as sole owner in the event of Mason's death. This last was Steve Hall's idea, inserted as the best guarantee of their confidence in Clee.

Betty Hall acted as one of the witnesses to the signing of the deed. More than once she regarded Clee in that same appraising, questioning manner of the night before, only today there was a challenging look in her glance, more mystifying to Clee than ever.

They came into the street after having left Mason at the hotel to await the arrival of the stage. As they stopped at the foot of the hotel steps, Betty suddenly turned to her father and said: "How about that letter to Matt Byne, Dad? You'd better let me get it in the mail before stage time."

The rancher reached inside his coat and brought out a letter. Clee, knowing that it must contain enough to name him guilty in what he had done, reached out and took it before the girl realized what he was doing.

"I've got a letter of my own to mail," he said, looking squarely at Hall and moving his head in a barely perceptible nod. "I'll mail yours along with mine."

Steve Hall thought he understood. Clee was using this as his excuse for leaving them to see Miles Banning, for the Catamount lay just beyond the hardware store that served as Wagon Fork's post office. So the rancher said to his daughter: "We'd better stick close to Art until he leaves."

"But Dad . . . !" Betty protested, a glow of anger deepening the olive tan of her cheeks. Abruptly

211

she turned to face Clee and blazed wrathfully: "You can carry this too far!"

Clee merely shrugged his shoulders and left them, hearing Hall rebuke the girl for her rudeness. Here was clear proof to Clee that Betty suspected him of what he had intended doing. Somehow she had learned of his betrayal of Matt Byne, but strangely enough she had not confided in her father.

He went to the post office—a wire cage at the rear of the hardware store—and bought a dime's worth of stamps, tucking Steve Hall's letter inside a pocket. From the hardware store he crossed to the county clerk's office, and there spent five minutes recording the deed to Art Mason's property.

Then, looking across at the Catamount, he thumbed out the butt of the Colt at his left thigh and started across the street toward the saloon. Sam, Banning's chief gun slick, was standing to one side of the batwing doors and noted his approach. Clee saw the man half turn and speak to someone inside, then resume his indolent posture against the frame wall of the building. There was no doubt but that Sam had relayed the news of Clee's arrival.

"The boss was expectin' you to drop in," Sam said easily, as Clee stopped in front of him. "Go right on up."

Clee thought he detected a trace of irony in the

man's tone, but put it aside as the gunman's reaction to the happenings of the day before. He entered the saloon to find it nearly empty. As he climbed the stairs, he was remembering the raid on Art Mason's place the night before, knowing that it had been Banning's work but was at a loss to explain the reason for the thing.

He knocked at the office door and heard the saloon owner's gruff voice bid him enter. As he opened the door, his first sight was of a sloping-shouldered, gray-eyed man in the chair alongside the desk. Banning sat behind it, his jowled countenance set soberly.

"Come in." Banning said silkily. "Come in and meet a friend of yours." The saloon owner indicated his visitor, and at the same time Clee noted the way the man wore his six-gun—at his left thigh, with the butt foremost. "Meet a gent who carries the same handle as yours," added Banning, "meet Gunnar King!"

It was like a blow in the face, and so entirely unexpected that for an instant Clee's surprise was reflected in his eyes. Then his face resumed its granite-like impassivity, and he covered his astonishment by a tight-lipped smile and drawled: "I wondered how soon you'd catch on, Banning."

Banning's hands had been resting in his lap, hidden by the desk. Now he raised them, and in one blunt fist he held a pearl-handled Smith & Wesson .44. He let it drop into line with Clee's shirt front and announced: "This isn't the first slug I've fired into the heart of a double-crosser."

Behind Clee, Sam stepped into the room, closing the door softly behind him and taking up his station to one side of it, his thumbs hooked in the belts close to his guns, his feet spread a little apart in a belligerent stance.

Clee's thoughts swirled madly, then settled to a calm reasoning that made him say: "You don't look like a fool, Banning. Better listen to what I have to say and then make up your mind about me."

Banning's lips curled down in a sneer. "The time for talk is over, brother."

Gunnar King, an unreadable set to his countenance, shifted his glance lazily to Banning and said: "No man would be loco enough to walk in here after what this gent has done unless he had something to say. I'd listen, Banning."

The saloon owner's thumb stubbornly drew back the hammer of his weapon. Its *click* was plainly audible as the catch snapped into place.

Clee said tonelessly: "Then you're throwin' over your one chance."

"What one chance?"

"You saw me ride in with Steve Hall. He's on his way now to get the sheriff. If I'm not out of here in ten minutes, they're coming in after me."

Slowly, so that his gesture could not be mistaken, Clee reached inside his shirt and brought out two tight rolls of bills, laying them on the desk as he said: "Here's five thousand dollars. It's to pay off Art Mason's note."

Banning sat dumbfounded, his weapon forgotten at this piece of insolence. Then, when he could summon words, he managed to say: "You think I'd let Mason pay off that note?"

"You'll have to. Yesterday a friend of Steve Hall's, a gent by the name of Matt Byne from up near Boston, sent him five thousand. This is it. He's sent me to pay off that note, and the sheriff knows it and will back him. You're out of it, Banning, out without a cent for all your trouble . . . unless you follow my play."

The saloon owner rocked his six-gun into position. "Let's have it . . . quick. Only give it to me straight this time, sidewinder."

Clee reached up and tapped the pocket of his vest. "I've got a deed here that makes me Art Mason's pardner. I thought you'd like a split."

Banning's eyes were wide in sheer disbelief. Abruptly Gunnar King's voice cut across the silence, suspicious, sharp-edged: "And why are you swingin' Banning in on something you could keep for yourself?"

Clee shifted his glance and met the outlaw's level stare unflinchingly. "I'm one against a dozen of you. Maybe I could stay alive for a while, but not long enough to cash in on the thing. This way, cuttin' you in on it, I can clean up enough for a decent grubstake and keep my hide whole. Another thing. This is to be a verbal agreement between us. I don't sign a thing over to you . . . in case you should decide later that I'd look good with a bullet in my back. So long as I'm alive, you'll get yours. If I die, you won't."

He disregarded Banning's leveled weapon as he stepped to the desk and leaned across it. "My share will be a third of this partnership. Split the rest any way you choose, but cut me in for a third or it's no pay."

Slowly, as he felt the weight of this argument, Miles Banning laid down the six-gun. "Your word had better be good," he said. "But let me get this straight. You've got a deed here that makes you Mason's pardner? How did you get him to sign it over to you?"

"I bought it with the money you paid me to dry-gulch Hall."

Banning's thick frame surged up out of the chair and his hand reached down for the gun again as a look of fury twisted his features.

"Wait!" Clee held up a hand. "It was the best I could do, Banning. Last night I found that Hall had enough money to pay off Mason's note and see him clear. That would have left us out of it . . . without a plugged nickel for our trouble. I'd told Steve Hall I was lookin' for a likely place to invest some money in land and cattle. So he put up the proposition for his friend . . . half ownership of Mason's layout if I'd furnish the money to get a mine started. Hall claims he's busted, so does Mason. It sounded square to me, and it was a sure chance for us to cash in. So I took it, seein' how we couldn't hog the whole thing."

Once again Gunnar King spoke. "He'll show you this deed if he isn't runnin' a sandy, boss."

Banning held out his hand, but Clee shook his head and drawled: "First you take this money and write me out a receipt and hand over Art Mason's note. I'll be in a tight spot with Steve Hall unless I can hand it over."

Banning looked at King, and the outlaw nodded. So the saloon owner faced about and opened the safe behind his chair. He reached into a drawer for a pen and ink, and with a succession of nervous flourishes he wrote out a receipt for $5,000 on the back of the note and endorsed it. Then, handing it to Clee, he said: "Now, let's see that deed."

Clee gave it to him and watched as he read the document. A smile erased Banning's scowl. "*Hm-m-m*. With Mason's death you fall into the whole thing," he mused. Suddenly a look of cunning blended with his smile and he muttered: "Blamed if I don't think you've swung a deal, friend. Look this over, King."

It wasn't until Gunnar King had finished reading the deed and had looked across at Banning with a wry smile wreathing his lean features that Clee had a hint of the harm he had done. He had thought the whole thing through—all but this. It was as though these men had spoken their thoughts aloud to him, and with realization of the chance he had given them, he heard Banning's words confirm his fears.

"Sam!" the saloon owner barked, jerking his head in the direction of the open window high on the wall behind his desk. "I heard the stage pull out two minutes ago. Art Mason's on it. You know what to do." He turned to the outlaw. "King, you go along and make sure it's a clean job."

An icy calmness took possession of Clee Adams then. "You're wrong again, Banning," he drawled. "Art Mason won't live for another month. He's sick, dyin'. The thing you're doing will only put the law after you. It won't take a yearling to guess who did the job, and why, if you gun Mason and burn the stage. Let him cash in his own way."

For a moment it looked as though his reasoning had carried. Then Miles Banning's face took on a flush and he snarled: "I told you once before I was goin' to get this town by the tail and make it mine. I've got what I want now, clear owner-ship of Mason's layout. And I've got guns to back me up. What I say goes from here on out." He looked at King and at Sam, and added: "Get goin'!"

Clee shrugged his shoulders, as though what Banning planned was of little importance.

Gunnar King rose from his chair and went out with Sam. As the door closed behind them, Clee said easily: "I hate to see a gent jump before he looks. Someday you'll remember what I told you, Banning."

He turned and was halfway across the room to the door when Banning called out sharply: "Hold it!"

Clee faced about to see that Banning again had the gun in his hand, leveled in exactly the same manner as before.

"You'll hang around until this is settled," Miles Banning muttered. "You've figured it out pretty well . . . about that deed and fixin' it so your hide is safe from a bushwhack. But I don't quite trust you, friend, even if you've bought me into something pretty big. We'll sit this out."

"And if Hall and the sheriff show up?"

"We'll just be sittin' here, havin' a good talk."

V

It wasn't five minutes later that a faint hope steadied Clee's frenzied thoughts. Art Mason's fate was sealed unless he could stop the stage ahead of Sam and Gunnar King, and, as he stared into the blunt snout of Banning's .44 and caught the cold gleam in the man's black eyes, even this one chance he had thought of a moment ago seemed a poor one.

"Are you forgettin' Steve Hall?" Clee queried.

Banning's look clouded.

Before the saloon owner could answer, Clee went on: "That's a real outfit of Hall's. Maybe I'll make a play for it myself, so long as you don't want it."

Banning was curious, although he tried to hide his interest behind a mask-like countenance. "The only reason I ever went against Hall was to get Mason's place," Banning said. "I've got Hall where I want him right now."

Clee shrugged his broad shoulders and turned his attention to the shaping of a cigarette.

As he touched a match to his cigarette, Banning queried: "What's on your mind?"

"Nothin'," Clee answered indifferently. He regarded Banning's menacing six-gun and added: "There was a time when I thought the two of us could make a cleanin' here." He shook his head regretfully. "Not now."

Banning glanced down at the weapon in his hand, as though noticing it for the first time. There was a two-second hesitation, in which the saloon owner obviously tried to master his greed. But then he laid the .44 on the desk before him, smiled, and said affably: "I wasn't any too sure about you. What the devil, a man can't take chances, with the stakes what they are this time. Maybe the two of us could do what you say . . . take over this country. What's that you were sayin' about Steve Hall?"

"Hall's got a girl, hasn't he?" Clee began, shifting his frame forward in his chair so that his hands were free. "And she's got the old man twisted around her little finger . . ."

Banning's full attention was centered on him, when suddenly Clee's right hand shot across his body and closed on the butt of his Colt. Banning made a frantic stab for his own weapon, but, before his hand could grip it, Clee's gun swiveled up in a streaking draw.

"I wouldn't, Banning," Clee drawled, coming up slowly out of his chair. He took two steps that put him in front of the desk, then reached down for Banning's weapon, and thrust it through the waistband of his Levi's.

The saloon owner's countenance blanched, and under the threat of that Colt he slowly raised his hands. Then, before he could dodge, Clee's gun rose and fell in a broad arc that ended in a hard blow alongside the saloon owner's right ear. Banning's hands fell lifelessly at his sides and he slumped down in his chair without a sound.

Clee remembered the deed to Mason's property, and took it off the desk and put it into his pocket along with the canceled note. Then, holstering his gun, he left the office. Below in the barroom, which was more crowded than when he had entered, he stopped long enough to tell a bartender: "The boss says he's not to be bothered for the next half hour."

Once outside, he glanced along the awninged walk in the direction of the hotel. Neither Steve Hall nor his daughter was in sight, so Clee walked openly to the hitch rail where his palomino was tied, and half a minute later he was in the saddle, spurring the animal at a hard run beyond the eastern limits of the town.

Art Mason missed the stage that afternoon. With the strange foreboding that sometimes warns men of their destiny, he had waited until they were about to carry him out of the hotel, and then had asked to speak to Steve Hall alone.

When the rancher was in the room with him, Mason said in a hollow voice: "It's no use, Steve. I wouldn't last twenty miles in the buckin' that stage would give me."

"What're you sayin'? You'll be on your feet again inside a month, Art."

Mason coughed hollowly, and Hall noted that his friend was paler than he had ever seen him. "I'm not goin', Steve. I haven't got much more time, and this is where I belong until I ride the river."

He put it bluntly, so that Steve Hall was at a loss for an answer. Nor could he find one as the seconds passed. At last he said lamely: "I'll go down and tell 'em you've decided to wait until tomorrow."

Half an hour later Art Mason asked for a doctor. When Steve had gone down to Doc Porter's office and brought him back to the hotel, Mason insisted that they leave him alone with the sawbones.

The rancher and his daughter went to the hotel porch and took chairs. A grim silence held them until the girl finally blurted: "Dad, what's happened to him?"

"Who, Art?"

"No. To this man Adams. He's been gone nearly an hour and a half. Where is he?"

Hall told the girl where Clee had gone, adding in a troubled tone, as he took out his watch and looked at it: "But you're right. He should have been back before now."

"Maybe he'll never come back . . . not until this is over with Art."

"What's botherin' you, Sis?"

In answer, Betty reached into a pocket of her jacket and handed her father Matt Byne's note. The rancher read it with his countenance taking on a grayish tinge. Suddenly he came to his feet and breathed: "So he's double-crossed us all. He's got a legal claim to that spread . . . if anything should happen to Art."

As though his words had been a prophecy,

Doc Porter came out through the hotel doors and strode hurriedly across to them. "Quick, Steve! Run down and get Belle Harkness. Art's just had a lung hemorrhage and needs a nurse."

Betty Hall choked back a sob and said: "Let me help, please."

The doctor looked at her gravely and said: "You'll do."

"Is there . . . will he come out of it?" Hall asked, his anger of a moment ago forgotten.

Porter merely shrugged his shoulders and lowered his eyes, muttering gruffly—"I'll have to be gettin' back to him."—and led the way inside, with Betty at his heels.

It was over quickly. Five minutes later Doc Porter pulled the sheet up over Mason's pillow, and Betty Hall met her father at the door to the room. "It's all over, Dad," she said softly.

Steve Hall's square jaw set in a hard line. For a long moment his stillness was a fitting tribute to his friend. Then, tonelessly, and in a voice that brought a rising alarm to his daughter's eyes, he said: "Art would have settled this the way I'm goin' to."

The palomino had held to a hard run for four miles when Clee saw the two riders a mile to the north of him as they climbed up over the top of a coulée. One rode a bay, the other a palomino.

They were riding in a direction opposite to his,

so he put them from his mind and once more leaned forward in the saddle and let the stallion feel the spur. Less than a minute later he shot a glance back along the trail to find that the two riders were cutting in, headed for town.

Suddenly he examined one of the horses fast disappearing behind him, a palomino, and tried to recognize the rider, for the first time remembering the horse Gunnar King rode. But it was the recognition of Sam's lean shape mounted on the bay beside the palomino that finally made Clee wheel his stallion about and head back along the trail. He was sure now that Banning's two men had already overtaken the stage and finished their grisly work.

The two ahead traveled fast, for Clee couldn't gain on them. So he let his animal settle into a canter, deciding that time no longer counted as it had minutes ago. He could settle this in town.

As he passed the first squat adobe of Wagon Fork, he pulled the stallion in to a walk. *No use stampedin' in,* he mused.

He pulled in warily at the hitch rail in front of the Catamount alongside the two ponies that had turned in there half a minute ago. Throwing the reins over the rail, he stepped up to the walk.

"Adams!" someone called out behind him. He looked across the street and saw Steve Hall striding down the opposite walk toward him. He raised a hand to the rancher and went on, thinking that whatever Steve Hall wanted could wait.

It came unexpectedly. He stepped in through the batwings and edged along the wall inside, so his eyes could become accustomed to the half light of the smoke-fogged room. Dimly, as though seen through a haze, he made out figures on the balcony. Three seconds later he recognized them as Sam and Gunnar King, supporting Banning's unsteady bulk between them. The saloon owner's white shirt was blood-matted at the shoulder from the wound on his head.

At the precise instant that Clee's vision cleared, he saw Banning weakly lift a hand and point down at him. King instantly released his hold on the saloon owner and stepped to the railing of the balcony, his right hand blurring across his body toward the weapon at his left thigh.

Clee pushed himself out from the wall and was conscious of the smooth, almost automatic play of the muscles in his right arm. His motion was timed exactly to the outlaw's, even to the upswing of the heavy Colt and the thumbing back of the hammer. Two guns blasted out in a single burst of thunder.

On the heels of that reverberating roar Clee winced from a sudden, searing pain low on his left side. He saw the buck of King's gun and saw the outlaw's body jerk spasmodically. Then King was frantically rocking his weapon into position again.

The crowd at the bar flattened to the floor as Clee thumbed back the hammer of his Colt and met Gunnar King's second blast with another flame-lancing shot. Even as the gun whipped back against the tension of his wrist, he saw the outlaw totter and reach out to grasp the railing in front of him. Then, slowly, as though his thick-set frame was an uprooted tree, Gunnar King fell out across the waist-high railing, lost his balance, and crashed down off the balcony to a poker table, splintering it like an egg crate.

Clee watched, fascinated, till across the sudden silence a second gun up there suddenly cut loose in two staccato blasts. A slug slapped into the wood alongside Clee's head. He glanced up to see Sam's tall frame hazed by a cloud of powder smoke.

Clee flattened out on the floor and rolled under the shelter of a nearby table as a third shot cut loose from Sam's weapon. Clee crawled along until he could see the gunman, then leveled his Colt, and thumbed two quick shots that beat Sam's body back against the pine-board wall above. The gunman's legs suddenly gave way under him and he slid to the balcony floor, his head sagging on his chest.

Clee threw open the loading gate and started punching the empties out of his gun. It was then that he heard Steve Hall's shout—"Watch Banning!"—from behind him at the doors.

It took Clee a full second to see Banning where he lay in the shadow on the balcony floor. The saloon owner had a gun in his hands, its snout thrust out between two of the railing posts.

Clee's gun was in his left hand, its loading gate open, and the hammer half cocked on an empty chamber. Banning had him at his mercy, for even a poor shot would have the time to aim and fire before Clee could spin the cylinder and bring his weapon into line.

Across the utter quiet Clee plainly heard the hammer click of Banning's weapon. But at that instant a dull-throated blast cut loose from behind Clee, and he saw Banning's hand jerk to one side and his gun drop clattering to the floor below.

Clee came to his knees and faced about to see Steve Hall, standing in the doorway with a smoking .45 hanging at his side.

"That was close," he breathed as he came to his feet. "Much obliged."

Hall's countenance was set in grim lines that remained even after Clee had spoken. "Maybe I ought to have let him shoot first, Adams. You might like to hear that Art Mason's dead and that you're owner of his layout now."

Clee nodded, saying lifelessly: "I tried to stop it, but they got there before I did."

It was as though Hall hadn't heard, for he said: "Art died at the hotel twenty minutes ago. I reckon you'll have some explainin' to do. Betty found that note of Matt Byne's in the money you gave me last night."

A man pushed through the doors behind Hall—the man who had first spoken to Clee on his coming to town, the sheriff. The lawman's glance swept the room and took in Gunnar King's body lying in the wreckage of the table at the rear. "Did Banning get it too, Steve?" he asked.

Mutely Steve Hall pointed above, to where Banning's white-shirted bulk lay in the shadows on the balcony. The sheriff saw, and smiled, and reached out to slap the rancher on the back. "I knew you'd do it, Steve. This clears things up the way I wanted."

Steve Hall protested, but others crowded in through the doors—others who hadn't seen the fight—and soon he was surrounded by a milling group of men who had waited for this showdown for months. They were mostly Steve's friends and now they mobbed him, whacking him on the back, pumping his hand, drowning out something he was trying to say.

Clee Adams had stepped to one side, closer to the doors. As the crowd thickened around Hall, he stepped unnoticed through the batwings and out to the walk.

Minutes later, Betty Hall ran up to her father, crying breathlessly: "I just heard about it, Dad!

Are you hurt?" Then, before he could answer, she went on in panic: "He rode out of town a minute ago."

"Who?" Steve Hall knew what her answer would be, for he had looked around a moment ago trying to catch sight of Clee Adams, only to discover that he had disappeared.

"Clee Adams. I thought you ought to know."

The crowd had quieted, realizing that something important was happening here. Steve Hall stood, wordless, undecided, when suddenly a white-shirted man wearing leather cuffs at his wrists and a green eyeshade on his forehead pushed his way inside the circle.

"I've been lookin' for you, Steve," he announced, holding out a paper in his hand. "Say, what did that gent mean by signing over Mason's property?"

Hall took the paper and saw at a glance that it was the deed they had drawn up two hours ago. His glance traveled down the page, to where he read the names of Matthew Byne and Steve Hall.

"When did this happen?" he asked hollowly.

"Less'n two minutes ago. This jasper Adams comes in and asks to change the recording of the deed. I couldn't find a thing wrong with it, knowin' that Art had passed away this afternoon. So I let him have his way. Then I got to thinkin' that it looked a bit queer. I thought you'd know."

For a long moment Steve's eyes sightlessly regarded the paper before him. Then he said humbly: "We had him figured wrong, Sis." Looking down, he saw with surprise that his daughter no longer stood beside him.

Out front, Betty untied a chestnut she had never seen before and climbed into the saddle. She guessed that Clee would be riding back along the trail he had taken in coming to Wagon Fork. She kicked the chestnut's flanks and sent the animal at a fast run out of town, a wild happiness leaping up in her as she recalled the clerk's words of a minute ago. Clee Adams was all man, after all.

Three miles beyond the end of the street she made out, far ahead, the rider on the palomino. Closer, she saw that his lean frame was weaving in the saddle. She used her reins to whip the chestnut and overtake the man she had so wrongly judged.

When they had stopped beside the trail, she took in the whiteness of his drawn face and saw the blood-matted side of his shirt. But there was something more important than this, and she put it into words.

"I was wrong about you, Clee. Can you . . . ?"

"No, you weren't wrong," was his toneless answer. "I came here to . . ."

She reined her horse closer to him and, reaching out, put her hand gently across his mouth. "Don't say it," she murmured. "The only

231

thing that matters is that you didn't do it, Clee. Would it make a difference if I wanted you to turn back?"

Some of the color crept back into Clee's angular face as sheer amazement wiped away his pain.

"You want me to come back?"

By way of answer, she leaned across and kissed him. Clee read in her eyes a promise that made him put from his mind the last shred of his past. Impulsively he gathered her in his arms, knowing then that his back trail had not betrayed him.

Showdown at Anchor

During the Second World War, Jonathan Glidden served in the U.S. Air Force Intelligence. When he returned to civilian life, he resumed his writing career where he had left off. Although he would continue to write Western fiction for the pulp magazines, in what was left of the 1940s four of his novels were serialized in *The Saturday Evening Post*. The present story was completed in early summer, 1947, and was sold to Popular Publications' *Fifteen Western Tales* on July 9, 1947. The author was paid $360 upon acceptance. The story appeared under the title "A Man for Hell's Canyon" in the issue dated November, 1947. For its appearance here both the title and text have been restored following the author's original typescript.

I

After that hard desert ride, Lodgepole looked clean and cool and quiet to Ed Nugent. The pines came right down and in among the cabins and grass, a bright emerald blanketing the wide banks of a clear-watered creek bisecting the single crooked street. The bridge spanning the stream was new, its timbers and planking a fresh-cut yellow. This morning's rain had laid the dust and washed things down and there was still a touch of its coolness in the sunny late afternoon.

Peaceful and tidy was Ed Nugent's thought after his first long look at the town. *The sort of place that would let a man take things easy.* That impression of his lasted exactly fifty-four minutes, no more, no less. During that short interval he helped a kid hostler at the livery barn rub down his brindle gelding and begin a careful feeding of the animal, played out after two days of fighting the desert's heat and wind-blown sand. Next he went to the barbershop and soaked his lean, long length in a tub of hot water, later letting the barber trim his dark hair, and then lying back to enjoy the luxury of a shave. He thought about going back to the stable and taking off the shell belt that sagged low at his flat thigh. In the end he decided against it, when the aroma of frying beef drew him into a restaurant along-side the barbershop. He downed a beefsteak and boiled potatoes, a dish of tomatoes, two wedges of dried-apple pie, and three cups of coffee.

As he paid for the meal, he bought a dime cigar, telling the man at the counter: "I'll be back in a couple of hours, for another go at that grub. It was good."

"Must take a lot to keep a man like you goin'." There was respect and some little awe in the clerk's answer. Aside from one man who frequently ate here, he couldn't remember ever having seen a taller one than this stranger.

Ed sauntered on up the street, pulling at the cigar, relaxed and feeling really good for the first time in a week. The trouble that had pushed him out across the desert seemed remote and unimportant now. Maybe he'd been a little hard on that gambler. Anyway, it would take a lot of healing before the cardsharp was on his feet again and the law would soon forget the name of Ed Nugent. He was here for a new start in a new country. He had a fair stake in his pocket and there was no hurry about finding work. He'd like to loaf right here for a day or two. Maybe tonight there would be a game down the street at the Congress Saloon worth his spending some time on. It wasn't the money that mattered, although he didn't like an empty pocket; it was the game that counted—fair cards and stakes high enough so a man

236

could back his hand or run a good lively bluff.

A rocker on the side verandah of the log hotel invited him and he climbed the steps and took the chair, cocking his spurs on the railing and watching the street take on more life now that evening was on its way. He saw two riders come down out of the pines and rack their horses at the rail fronting the Congress. A dignified man in a black suit came out of the bank, locking the door, and then went into the Mercantile, to reappear shortly, carrying a sack of groceries under his arm, his dignity still with him. A shad-bellied oldster wearing a nickel star on his vest walked up the street and past the hotel, looking up at him and nodding pleasantly. Ed was feeling good enough to drawl: " 'Evening, Sheriff."

Yes, this was a choice spot. A man could put down roots in a place like this and never want for much. The people were friendly. The range he had ridden at midday was rich and there must be a good bit more of it tucked back in the folds of these near foothills. He was wondering about the price of land when a buckboard headed up the street toward him to interrupt his wondering.

A medium-built man with pale blond hair was holding the reins and a rare piece of horseflesh, a light-saddled bay, was tied to the end gate and trotted after the rig. But it was the girl sitting alongside the driver who finally took Ed's eye and held it.

When the buckboard turned in at the rail beyond the verandah, he had the chance to prove correct his first impression that the girl was something even rarer than the bay. She stepped lightly down off the wheel hub, smiling at the blond man who gave her his hand. Ed had never seen blue- and white-checked calico look so expensive and stylish. Her dress was full-skirted and gathered tightly at a slender waist, snug enough to give the strong hint of a supple, slender figure. She was hatless and wore her corn-silk hair high-piled on her head. Her face possessed a quality that went beyond prettiness, so that Ed noticed its strength and vivaciousness before the fine molding of the features caught his eye. He was thinking he had never seen eyes a deeper blue than hers as she came on up the steps and past him.

Because he was unashamedly looking at her, he noticed the way she stopped just short of the door and, a frightened look crossing her face, turned quickly, and said: "Don't come up here, Sam."

Her words came too late, stopping her spare-bodied companion on the top step. Three men were already on the way out the door, passing the girl, the one in the lead having to duck his head and hunch his massive shoulders to clear the door frame. He was probably the biggest man Ed had ever come across—he was, in fact, the one the restaurant clerk had been thinking about—

and everything about him was oversize, his height and breadth and thickness.

The big man said tonelessly: "Better go on in, Laura." He wasn't looking at the girl as he spoke. His pale gray eyes were on Sam. Ed saw the girl stiffen and anger flared brightly in her eyes. "Don't, Tom," she breathed. Then, when the big man paid her not the slightest attention, starting on out for the blond cowpuncher, she said more loudly: "Tom, I order you to go straight back in there."

That stopped the big one. His hard glance shuttled from Sam to the girl. "Any other time I'd listen, Laura," he said with a strong respect in his tone. "But your father sent us here to do what we're doin'."

"Dad can't lord it over everybody like . . ."

The massive Tom was already taking another step away from her, not listening. Ed's careful glance took in Sam now and what he saw filled him with admiration and a strong measure of pity. The young blond man was almost a full head shorter than Tom. Yet his deeply tanned face showed not the slightest trace of fear. Instead, his expression was dogged, even defiant. He wore no weapon Ed could see. His arms were cocked, fists doubled, and a blaze of hatred touched the glance he focused on the big man.

The girl, seeing her words having no effect, suddenly ran out and caught a hold on Tom's arm.

Ed sat straight in the chair as the big man lazily swept his arm down, breaking her hold easily. "Keep her back, Briggs," Tom drawled, and one of the other pair, a gangling scarecrow of a man, came out and took the girl by the elbow, pulling her away as Tom added: "Sandy, put a gun on him."

The remaining man in the trio deliberately drew a Colt from his belt and lined it at Sam, who so far hadn't spoken or moved a muscle. The girl suddenly pulled free of Briggs's hold and started in at Tom again. The way the big man swung his arm, brushing her roughly aside, brought Ed up out of his chair.

Tom seemed to have been expecting some such thing, for his arm came on around and his hand jarred Ed's shoulder hard, bowling him back down into the chair with such force that one of the rockers snapped, cocking the chair aslant. He gave Ed a brief chill look, saying almost gently: "Stay out o' this, stranger."

He stepped out at Sam once more and Sandy, the one with the drawn .45, moved closer in behind Ed's chair. Sam stood his ground, smiling faintly as though knowing that what was coming was inevitable and that there was no use in wasting effort dodging it.

"You had your warnin', Sam," Tom said an instant before he swung.

At the last split second Sam ducked his head

and hunched a shoulder. He should easily have avoided the blow, for Tom wasn't particularly fast. But the ham-like fist slammed into Sam's shoulder and rocked him back on his heels. He tried to catch himself. He was too close to the porch's edge. His boot reached into thin air and he did an ungainly backward cartwheel, hitting the middle step on his hip and going on over. When he lay sprawled on the walk, he tried to push up, then fell back again with a stunned and baffled look of pain crossing his face.

"Go get him, Matt. Bring him up here." Tom stood with fists planted on his hips, looking down at Sam. There was no pity in his dark eyes.

Briggs let go of the girl and went down the steps and hauled Sam to his feet again. The girl cried: "Stop! Can't you see he's hurt?" She tried to come on past Tom once more, but with that easy swing of his arm he swept her back toward the door.

This huge man, Ed was thinking, had the broadest back and the most powerful pair of shoulders he had ever seen. Something was going on here that he realized wasn't strictly his affair. But he had never seen a man push a woman around this way and it wasn't right. It was so wrong that he wondered what would happen now if he tried to stand again. He looked around, saw the bore of the .45 lined at him, and, over his boiling rage, decided to stay as he was.

Briggs dragged the dazed Sam on up the steps, and, when they stood there at the edge of the porch, Tom drawled: "Hold him up."

Briggs lifted Sam erect and pinned his arms behind him. Tom stepped in deliberately and hit him. This time he connected solidly. Sam's head snapped back, dropped to his chest. Tom struck again and again, smashing Sam's nose, cutting open his lips.

The girl screamed and her cry caught Sandy's attention briefly. His eyes had barely moved from Ed before Ed was lunging up. Tom half turned then toward the girl and Ed. Sandy saw what was coming and started bringing the .45 around again. But Ed's Colt blurred up, exploded, and Sandy's .45 spun to the boards as he grunted with pain, clamping left hand to his sprung wrist.

Tom wheeled warily around, forgetting the unconscious Sam.

Ed Nugent nodded down to Sandy's weapon that lay close at the girl's feet. "Miss," he drawled, "if you want some fun, hold that on these gents while I get to work."

Her wide, frightened eyes were puzzled for only a moment before she snatched up the Colt, cocked it, and pointed it at Tom. She said: "Tom Hale, I'm going to cripple you. I'm going to . . ."

"Hold on," Ed cut in quietly. "This is my party. Just keep 'em off my back." He stepped in on Tom Hale and flipped the man's Colt from holster, tossing it out across the walk.

Briggs let go his hold on Sam and lifted his hands. Sam slumped to the floor, half curled up like he was sleeping. Briggs's .44 arched out and landed beside the big man's in the drying mud at the walk's edge. Ed dropped his own weapon back into holster and suddenly threw a stiff jab at the big man's face. It happened so quickly that neither Tom nor the girl was expecting the blow. She had started to say something as Tom Hale's head rocked back on his thick neck. Then a look of gladness came to her eyes and she moved her weapon around so that it covered both Briggs and Sandy, who had stepped well clear of Ed now.

That first punch shook Tom Hale but didn't hurt him. Hard on the heels of it he threw a vicious roundhouse swing that would have knocked Ed all the way to the walk had it connected. Ed simply ducked under it and rose with all the weight of his ropy-muscled shoulders behind a fist that buried itself just above the big man's belt. Hale gagged and doubled over. Then Ed's other fist jarred him erect with a solid impact on the point of the jaw. Pain lanced through Ed's knuckles and wrist and he drew back as Hale groped out wildly trying to reach him. When the pain eased off, Ed stepped in again, knocking aside the man's thick arms, then slashing his knuckles across the wide mouth. A look of bewilderment crossed Hale's face as the blood ran down his chin.

Ed hit him once more, fully on the jaw hinge.

The verandah railing was a long pine pole braced by cross pieces at three places. Several men could sit on it and it would sag but never crack. Hale's crumpling weight hit it and the whole railing tore loose and one end of it fell into a pair of onlookers who had come running up at the sound of the shot a few seconds ago. They stumbled out of the way as Tom Hale hit the walk planks on his back and rolled over, trying to stand.

Ed jumped down and helped Hale to his feet, then stepped back, and threw a sure uppercut that flattened the big man's nose and buckled his knees. As Tom Hale went down the second time, Ed turned and glanced to the porch, aware now that several men stood close by on the walk, watching. He caught the girl's eye. "Enough, miss? That makes it about even, except that they knocked your friend out. Want me to put this moose to sleep?"

"No . . . you've done enough." The girl was pale and her look frightened. She no longer held up the Colt. It hung at her side.

Ed eyed Briggs and Sandy. "Better heft your sidekick in off the walk," he drawled. "He's big enough to be in the way."

Meekly, not looking at Ed, they came on down the steps and out to Hale, trying to lift him to his feet and making a clumsy job of it. Finally they had him erect between them and were walking out through the crowd and down the walk, the gathering crowd stepping aside for them.

Ed saw the sheriff push his way in through the onlookers and had the idle thought—*Peaceful, was it?*—before the lawman stopped two strides short of him, wanting to know: "What did you do to Hale?"

"What Tom deserved to have done to him, Sheriff!" called the girl, coming to the edge of the porch. "He and those two others half killed Sam Richards. Someone had better get him up to the doctor's."

There was a lot of talk then, and the sheriff seemed to have forgotten Ed as he came on past him and climbed the steps to kneel alongside the unconscious Sam. Ed sauntered on down the walk. He crossed to the far side of the street a few buildings below, headed for the livery barn— headed on out of the country, he supposed.

But by the time he was lugging his saddle into the stall where the brindle stood, a stubborn anger was rising in him. He'd done nothing the law could hold him for. The brindle needed rest and so did he. How did it happen he was running again? He took the saddle back and slung it over the pole and went on up the street in the gathering dusk. The crowds had shifted to the walk in front of a building, several doors above the hotel. The verandah rail still lay there on the planks and Hale and his two men were nowhere in sight. Ed paid no attention to several idlers across the street who watched him go into the hotel.

The small lobby was deserted and nearly dark. He lit a lamp on the desk at the foot of the stairs, signed the book there, took a key from the board behind the railing, and went on up to Room 6, wondering how long it would take the sheriff to track him down.

It took even less time than Ed thought it would. The gray twilight was only beginning to thicken at the window—and he had barely half smoked a cigarette, lying stretched on the bed in the darkening room—when the solid clump of boots sounded along the hallway. He pushed up onto an elbow, instinct running his hand to the Colt. But then he thought better of the move and lay back again. When the door of his room swung abruptly open, he had his hands laced behind his head.

In the faint light he recognized the sheriff and drawled: "You're old enough to have picked up the habit of knockin', friend."

"So I am."

The door slammed shut with a violence that rattled the raised sash of the window. The lawman went to the washstand and lit the ornate lamp sitting on it. As he put the rose-glass shade back onto its holder, he faced Ed with a stern look on his narrow face. "Who are you and what're you doin' here?"

"The handle's Ed, Sheriff. And I'm tending my own knittin', doing just as little as will get me by."

"You'd better talk, mister," the lawman said sharply. "Did Sam Richards pay to bring you in here to make that play against Hale?"

Ed solemnly shook his head, saying owlishly: "That's between me and Richards."

"They say you're real slick with that Forty-Five. So you admit Sam brought you in?"

Ed swung his boots off the bed, sitting up. "That's what you want, isn't it?"

"Ever see Sam Richards before?"

"No."

"Ever been here before?"

Ed shook his head, pinching the end of his smoke, and tossing it out the window.

The sheriff's testy manner faded before a harassed look. "I believe you," he said with a surprising frankness. "The reason I do is that no man knowing the way the cards are stacked here would have dared to do what you did. You must've walked into it blind." Ed sat, waiting for more. It came shortly. "You've got maybe two hours before Hale gets back here with Anchor's crew. He'll hunt you down if he has to take this town apart."

"Why?"

"Why?" the lawman echoed incredulously. "Don't you know what you did?"

"Whittled an overstuffed jasper down to his right size."

"Man, no one's ever so much as lifted a hand against Anchor. Against John Worth or his ramrod."

"Somebody was liable to, someday."

The sheriff's look was completely baffled now. He sighed deeply, shaking his head. "So you did. The Lord knows how you got away with it. You were plain lucky. But now's not the time to crowd your luck. You'll have to get out."

Ed seemed not to have heard as he drawled: "So that's her name. Laura Worth."

The lawman halfway read Ed's thought, for he said quickly: "You buy into her game, mister, and you'll think you never saw trouble. She's bucking her father . . . and no one does that."

"You've said that twice now, Sheriff."

"And I'll say it again. The . . ."

His words broke off as a light knock came at the door. Ed called—"Come in."—and stood up off the bed as the door opened.

It was Laura Worth. She was even prettier than Ed had thought. She was away from violence, lamplight laying a soft shadow across her face that gave it a mysterious, haunting beauty. Her direct eyes moved from Ed to the lawman and a faint smile touched her expression. "I knew you were here, Bob. I wanted to see both of you."

The sheriff said helplessly, angrily, yet with an affection beneath his tone Ed didn't miss: "Haven't you stirred things up enough for one day?"

"I can thank this man for what he did for Sam,

can't I?" she asked, a mischievous look coming to her eyes.

"Thank him and then get out."

"And if he isn't working, I can offer him a job, can't I?" Her tone was mock-innocent. She looked at Ed. "Would you take a riding job? Even if Sheriff Coombs says you shouldn't?"

"Laura, listen," the lawman breathed. "What's between your father and Sam Richards isn't your affair. Let it alone. Keep out of it."

"I happen to be very fond of Sam," she said evenly. "And I happen to think my father is beyond his rights in what he's doing. I'm of age. Six months over, in fact. I have every right to take sides in this."

"John Worth won't let anything get in his way now, family or no family," Coombs intoned gravely. "Laura, this is a grown-up game they're playing. Someone may get hurt."

"Which reminds me, Bob. What are you doing to stop it? What legal right does Dad have for beating up a man simply because he's seen with me?"

Coombs's face reddened and he was groping for a reply when Ed drawled: "I'll listen, miss. But I'd have to know more about it."

"You will," the girl told him.

Coombs said resignedly: "Then tell it all. If he knows everything, he won't touch it with a California rope."

"Two months ago Sam Richards was working for my father as a wrangler," Laura Worth said, ignoring the sheriff's comment. "He'd been with us for over a year and done well with the job. Then one day Dad sent him up north to bring down a batch of horses Tom Hale had bought for Anchor at an auction up there. Some sort of business delayed Hale, and Sam set out alone with the horses. The first night several riders hit his camp and stampeded the horses. Sam lost every animal. When Hale heard about it, he told Dad he'd seen Sam talking to Len Avery and . . ."

"Len Avery's a renegade white livin' on the reservation east of here." The sheriff inserted his words dryly, with a thinly veiled meaning. "Every time those bucks break out and go on one of their sprees, Avery's with 'em. He's a rustler, a petty thief, and a squaw man among other things. Worth fired Sam, same's anybody would, and Laura horned in."

"Of course I did." Her eyes were bright with defiance now. "I was sorry for Sam, ashamed of the way he'd been treated."

"You didn't have to stake him, loan him that money."

"In my place you'd have done the same thing, Bob Coombs," Laura flared.

"What money?" Ed asked, seeing the conversation going beyond him.

"Money to buy eight sections of land the

government was selling after a resurvey of the reservation's west line," the girl told him. "Sam and I knew it was up for sale by sealed bids. We knew Dad had talked Tom Hale into making a bid on it. We even knew what Tom's bid was to be. So I loaned Sam the money to buy it."

"At exactly a hundred more than Hale had offered," the sheriff prompted.

"Yes." There was a proud touch to Laura Worth's expression now. "So Sam got the land and moved onto it. Dad was furious. He forbade me to see any more of Sam. Yesterday we had it out, Dad and I. I won't have him telling me what I can and can't do. So I brought some things into town and I'm living here now at the hotel. As soon as he learns he can't bully decent men, I'll go back to Anchor." Ed liked the way Laura Worth lifted her shoulders, as her glance came around to him again. "So there you have it. Most of it, anyway. Well, what's your answer? Do you want a job with Sam, knowing all this?"

Ed thought it over deliberately, drawling finally: "Why not? When do I start?"

A look of gladness lighted her face. "Tonight. We'll head for the Triangle as soon as I've changed."

"You'll damn' soon regret it if you do, son," the sheriff said very soberly.

251

II

She had agreed to meet him at the livery, asking him to have a horse saddled for her, and, when she came down along the dark, awninged walk, he saw that she was still bareheaded but had changed from the dress to a man's outfit—flannel shirt, denim jumper, and waist overalls. The boots made her tall enough, so that the top of her head was well above his shoulder as she came in alongside him and took the reins of her sorrel.

Neither of them said anything as she led the way down the street and, well out past the last cabin, took a climbing trail that forked north from the road. They were riding through the pines before they had gone another 100 yards, and, as the deep obscurity closed about them, she slowed the sorrel out of a trot to let him come alongside.

"We'll take our time," she said. "Your animal's seen some travel lately."

It wasn't a question but he saw it as one, knowing she must have gone to the stable earlier and inspected the brindle, for she couldn't have noticed what she mentioned in this darkness.

"He brought me across from Chimney yesterday and the day before," Ed told her.

He could barely make out her face turning abruptly toward him. There was a quality of strong surprise in her voice as she asked: "In only the two days?"

"And part of last night. We were both thirsty."

"You must have been in a hurry. That's a four-day ride at this season."

He grinned broadly, knowing she couldn't see. "Wanted to get it over with."

She had nothing to say to that. But presently, as they dipped across a grassy swale circled by the pines, she asked: "Are you as good with a gun as they said you were when you caught Sandy so flatfooted?" There was a brief silence before she went on: "I'm not trying to pry. It's only that I want to be sure you can help Sam."

"Gun help?"

She was a long time in answering. When she spoke, her voice was low, dead serious. "Yes, I suppose that's it. And yet, Sam Richards really doesn't mean much to me . . . only this is his chance, the chance of a lifetime to build up a place of his own. He wanted that when he came into this country. I couldn't . . . won't let Dad ruin him."

They rode on in silence for some minutes, Ed trying to figure why he had let her talk him into taking this job with Sam Richards. He had crossed the desert to ride clear of trouble, to stay clear, and here he was headed into more. *Chasing a petticoat?* he asked himself, and at once decided—*that's not all of it. . . .*—stubbornly

253

refusing to admit that anyone, man or woman, had enough influence over him to make him give up any measure of his carefree independence. His siding Sam Richards had been a normal reaction to take up with the underdog—and there had been a clean and honest look about the wrangler, a courageous stubbornness that even now played on his feeling for fairness.

"You haven't yet told me your name," Laura said, breaking a long run of silence between them.

"Nugent. Ed Nugent."

"That's a new one," she said. "There's a nice sound to it."

She didn't press more questions on him and he was grateful for that. When next she spoke again, minutes later, her words packed a measure of surprise. For she said: "Promise me just one thing, Ed. I don't mind Dad's having to eat crow. Anchor's been too high and mighty for too long. And he's wrong in backing Tom Hale the way he does. But I wouldn't want . . . well, I just don't want anything to happen to him."

"Then he'd better stay out of Sam Richards's way."

"I hope he will, but it's not as simple as that. Sam picked up a bunch of culls the agent rejected from the reservation herd. Dad wants them kept off his range and that's been impossible. Sam and Al Abbot, the man he's got working for him, have been stringing wire as fast as they can, but it takes time to fence in eight sections. Meantime, Sam's beef's been drifting over onto Anchor grass. And Dad keeps insisting on a tie-up between Sam and this Len Avery. If any Anchor stock disappears from now on, he'll blame it on Sam."

"Any chance that Sam was in with Avery stealing those horses?"

"Not any, Ed. Can't you tell an honest man when you see one?"

He nodded, drawling: "Sometimes. But here's a thing I don't *sabe*. If this Avery's a known rustler, why don't they string him up?"

"They've never proved anything. The beef that's run off this slope usually goes through the reservation's west fence and cuts north into the next county. By the time arrangements are made with the agent to look for the cattle, they've simply disappeared. There are ranchers up in that country who aren't too particular about brands. And for some reason the law up there has never co-operated with Bob Coombs."

They were riding up a steep and rocky cañon now and for a time the clatter of their horses' shoes was a racket they couldn't talk over. Within a half mile the cañon floor began gradually leveling out and the rims fell away across a broad expanse of grass that showed indistinctly in the starlight.

Laura said: "Here's the start of Triangle." She was silent a moment, then added quietly, feelingly: "Ed, that promise you're giving doesn't hold for Tom Hale. He's mostly what's wrong with Dad. Sometimes I wish something could happen to him."

Ed didn't answer and for a quarter minute their animals walked side-by-side, the squeak of leather and the slur of hoofs brushing through the fetlock-deep grass was the only sound breaking the stillness.

"Ed, you haven't given your promise," Laura reminded him.

"I'm thinking maybe I'd better ride on out of the whole thing."

She looked across at him, trying to read some expression in the dark outline of his face. "I hope you don't," she said finally, with a directness that jolted him and faintly stirred his anger.

"You can't put a rein like that on a man," he said in a brittle voice. "Suppose your father does decide to push Sam out. Suppose he has his chance at either Sam or me. Are we to unbutton our shirts to give him an open shot at our ribs and not do anything about it?"

"No, Ed." Her voice was barely above a whisper. "But I'd want you to . . . just do what you can for Dad."

"That I can promise," he said.

"Maybe he won't ask for trouble."

And maybe he will, was Ed's thought as they rode on.

• • •

Stringing fence for another man was something Ed Nugent hadn't thought he would ever be doing again. He had drawn top wages at every outfit he had worked for over the past five years— since he had turned twenty—and had bossed fence crews, but never handled the wire himself. Now he was doing exactly that, gouging his hands raw even though he wore thick leather gloves. He and Al Abbot, Sam's crewman, had dug more post holes and rolled out more spools of wire in the past two days than he cared to remember. His arm and back muscles were stiff and he wasn't used to being afoot so much.

Yet he didn't begrudge even one minute of the long, hard hours he had put in for Sam Richards. Sam hadn't stirred from the cabin during these two days, couldn't. His dislocated hip wouldn't carry his weight and Ed wasn't at all sure that the wrangler's jaw wasn't broken. Sam couldn't open his mouth to take in much food, let alone chew it. Yesterday Laura had come out from town and made up a stew for him, and this morning he had seemed a little stronger, his spirits better.

At sundown they had finished dropping a load of spools along the north line of new cedar posts and were riding the buckboard down across a meadow a mile below in the direction of the cabin. Al was drawling: "My guts are gnawin' bad enough to take even my own cookin'. We'll fry up some steaks and have a real feed."

"Wish Sam could chew a chunk of it." Ed slapped the team with reins to lift them to a faster trot.

"There's a good man." Al's long face was set seriously. "It's a funny thing about him, though. He's different now."

"How?"

"That bustin' up he took put vinegar into him, 'stead of takin' it out like it was supposed to. Remember what he said to the girl the other night when she brought you up here?"

Ed nodded, remembering well. Laura had asked Sam how he was feeling, if his hip hurt much, and he had answered: "This is the best thing that could have happened to me. This afternoon I was half of a mind to pull out, leave for good. Now I'm here to stay." The flinty look in his gray eyes had been even more eloquent of his feelings than his words. But then his look had softened as he spoke again to Laura. "You'd better keep clear of this from now on . . . it's gone too far for a woman to have anything to do with it." Such talk, coming from as mild-looking a man as Sam, had left its impression on Ed. He remembered how Laura's face had paled as she took in the full meaning of what he had said, as though she had just then realized for the first time how deadly serious this trouble might become.

"That girl now," Al went on, interrupting Ed's thoughts. "Damned if I can figure her out, goin' against her own flesh and blood this way. Someone's likely to get hurt."

"She's proud," Ed said, "and maybe ashamed at seeing how hog-wild her old man's gone. But she can't back out now an' hold her head up."

Al frowned. "Suppose that's it. Puts me in mind of how mad I once got when my pappy whaled the livin' daylight out of a nester that run his critters across our place. Small man, the sod-buster was, gettin' up in years. There wasn't nothin' right about it."

They were in among the trees now, the cabin in sight below. Blue cedar smoke drifted lazily from the chimney, fanning out across the wide bay in the timber. They came abreast the corral and Ed reined in the team.

They were unharnessing when Al suddenly breathed a low oath and said softly, sharply: "Over your right shoulder, Ed."

Looking that way, Ed saw big Tom Hale step into the open from behind the corral fifty feet away. Cradled across the crook of the Anchor ramrod's arm was a double-barreled shotgun. Ed turned to face the man, startled with a strong sense of fore-boding in him. He wasn't wearing his Colt. A Winchester lying in the buckboard bed was the only weapon he and Al had taken with them this morning. So now he didn't even bother lifting his hands.

A slow, satisfied smile patterned Hale's square face, twisting his still-swollen lips in an odd way. "The party's over, gents!" he called. "Just move over this way . . . careful."

Suddenly from behind him, Ed heard the pound of Al's boots on the far side of the team. He called loudly—"Don't, Al!"—as he read the meaning of that sound. Al was making a break for it.

Tom Hale stopped and raised the shotgun to his shoulder. It cut loose its thunder, with rosy flame stabbing from both barrels. On the heels of the deafening explosion came Al's hoarse scream.

Ed wheeled and looked beyond the team. Al lay sprawled brokenly on the ground off toward the trees. Even though Hale called sharply—"You, Nugent! Stay set!"—Ed walked over there.

One look was enough to fill Ed with a cold rage. The double load of buckshot had caught Al between the shoulders. The sight sickened him. He quickly pulled off his jumper, spreading it across the upper part of the body, and then faced Hale once more.

"You blood-hungry fool! You've killed him."

Hale spoke calmly. "Get in there with Richards."

Ed for the first time noticed Matt Briggs's lanky frame leaning in the doorway of the cabin. A moment later Sam Richards appeared beyond the Anchor man and hobbled on past him before Briggs caught him and pulled him back in through the door again.

"Come on, get movin'," Hale drawled.

Ed was warned to obey by the cool tone of the man's voice and by the thing he had just witnessed. He went on around the corral, hearing Hale's step coming along behind him. Briggs moved back out of the doorway, and, when Ed stepped in, it was to find Sam sitting on his bed, his battered face drained of color and a baffled rage showing in his eyes.

"He killed him," Sam said in a lifeless voice.

Ed nodded. "But why, Sam?"

"Why? We're rustlers," Sam told him, his voice strong and acid with anger now. "We ran off a herd of Anchor beef last night. Pushed it onto the reservation. They say we've made a deal with that one-armed Avery to take the herd off our hands."

"Remember the tracks, Richards," Briggs drawled across the momentary silence.

Sam laughed, a hysterical note in his voice. "Ed, they say they followed our sign straight back here from the break in the reservation fence." He suddenly stood up, stumbling as he forgot and put weight on his bad leg. "Damn it, Ed! Tell 'em we didn't stir from here last night!"

"Save it to tell the sheriff," came Hale's voice from the doorway behind Ed. "Matt, go get the horses."

Briggs moved around Ed and out the door. Ed turned to Hale, asking: "Why didn't you bring your sheriff along?"

"Waste all that time to town and lettin' you three get away? Uhn-uh!"

"If we were making a getaway, why didn't we do it last night?"

"Damned if I know," Hale said evenly. "You must've thought you'd hid your sign better'n you had."

All at once Sam was saying urgently: "Ed, remember last night when you thought the horses were actin' up down at the corral?"

Ed nodded. He had left his blankets and gone out to the corral in the middle of the night, curious at hearing the horses moving around. But by the time he had walked down there, the animals had already quieted and he had seen nothing wrong.

"Ed, did you rub down your horse when you finished work last night?" Sam went on insistently.

"Sure. I always do."

A gleam of satisfaction came to Sam's eyes now as he looked at Tom Hale. "I went down there to the corral this mornin', just for something to

do. After you and Al left, Ed. The hair on your brindle's back was matted down like you'd forgotten to curry him. He was ridden last night. After you finished with him."

A slow inscrutability had settled over Hale's face.

"You get it, Ed?" Sam's voice was trembling now. "They took our horses after we turned in and rode 'em up there to where the herd went through, then brought 'em back. You heard something going on at the corral. It must've been them turnin' the horses in again. Now they say they've got sign to prove we ran the herd off."

Ed was watching Hale. No flicker of expression showed on the Anchor man's face as he drawled: "Save that for Coombs, too, Richards. We're taking you in. Only don't plan on Coombs's swallowin' a story like that."

Sam Richards's temper finally snapped. He began putting every name he could think of to Hale, who listened for several moments, and then leisurely walked over and knocked him back onto the bed with a gun butt.

Sam's mouth was still bleeding when they carried him out and roped him onto his saddle ten minutes later. Shortly they did the same with Ed. Dusk was settling in through the pines as they took the town trail, Hale leading the way. Behind the Anchor foreman, Sam rode crookedly, leaning away from his bad leg. Ed stayed close to Sam's rear, ready to ride alongside and shoulder him erect if he lost his balance. Briggs came last, riding leisurely. For the most part they were silent.

Once or twice Ed heard Sam muttering to himself. He was close to the breaking point and Ed himself was a little awed. The evidence against them would be hard to argue against. Sam Richards's name in town was not too good at best. Being included as a victim of this circumstance didn't particularly worry Ed, simply because he wouldn't let himself think about it.

As they left the high grassy bench and headed down through the darkness into the cañon Ed had two nights ago traveled with Laura, he began guiding the gelding in and out between the boulders by a touch of the spur. He had trained the brindle to obey that prod. Now it was saving him from an uncomfortable ride. Time and again Sam, up ahead, was badly jolted as his horse took the hard going without a hand on the reins to guide him over the worst of it.

They were coming abreast a narrow brush-choked off-shoot when Ed abruptly thought of something that made him turn and look behind. He couldn't see Matt Briggs, but the man was back there, somewhere in the darkness. He could hear the steady hoof strikes of Briggs's horse sounding against the cañon's rocky floor. Up ahead, Tom Hale's massive shape made a dense shadow against the blackness. Every few minutes, as long as it was light, Ed had noticed Hale turning to look back at them.

Hale might be watching, but Ed weighed that

chance and decided to take it as he touched the gelding's flank with the spur of his left boot. The brindle swung over to the right, its pace a steady slow walk. The thicket loomed close in front of Ed and a touch of the right spur, then another of the left, put the gelding around the thicket's edge and into the mouth of the narrowing cleft angling deeply into the wall.

At the last moment Ed decided against riding out this small side cañon, knowing he risked being boxed and having them hunt him down, probably to kill him. He put his horse straight in at the wall behind the thicket. The animal stopped a stride short of the sheer-climbing rock and came to a stand.

Ed listened warily, breathing shallowly, his nerves drawn wire-tight. Gradually he made out the sound of Sam's horse going away. Then the hoof thud of Briggs's animal lifted over other sounds as Briggs drew abreast and continued steadily on.

Suddenly Tom Hale's voice came to him faintly calling: "Close in, Matt! We got to make time."

He would have to play his chance for all it was worth. He turned the gelding out into the cañon, again using the spur. He managed to get the animal started back the way they had come. Suddenly Matt Briggs's strident shout echoed up to him. He rammed home both spurs and the startled gelding lunged into a run.

III

The first news of the hunt reached Lodgepole at mid-afternoon of the next day when a posse man, Nels Baker, having to catch the evening stage on important business, rode back to town. Ed Nugent was still at large.

"This bird, Nugent," Baker told the crowd that gathered at the sheriff's office, "fooled the pack of us. Where would be the last place you'd expect to find him?"

"Anchor!" someone called out, and there were a few guffaws.

Another man made a guess. "Sam Richards's place."

"Right," Baker said. "Damned if he hadn't gone back there, and dug a grave and buried Abbot, sacked himself some grub, and just rode away. Hale claims there was two Forty-Fives in the cabin and a Winchester lyin' in the buckboard. Nugent's luggin' all three."

"Where'd he go from there?" one of the listeners wanted to know.

Baker shrugged tiredly. "They're up there along the *malpais* now, thrashin' around, tryin' to spot where he come out of all that rock. Coombs is bringin' Sam on down in another hour or two."

Laura Worth stood along the walk at the back

266

fringe of the crowd. Now she stopped holding her breath, gladness running through her as she turned and walked away. *They'll never get him!* she told herself. But the next moment her fears crowded in on her again.

She was climbing the hotel steps, wholly engrossed by her thoughts of Ed, before she saw her father. John Worth had risen from a chair on the verandah and now stood waiting for her alongside the mended rail. She stopped and stood irresolutely, before her pride steadied her and carried her on.

"Laura, I'd like a word with you," the rancher said quietly as she reached the head of the steps.

"There's nothing you can say that will help now." She wanted to walk on past him. But a certain humility written on his face puzzled her, made her curious enough to linger in hope of finding out what backed it.

"I can say this, child," he told her gravely. "I never thought this would come to killing."

"Your own men are the only ones who have done any killing so far, Dad. You should be proud of Tom Hale."

She could see him wince, but that strange humility stayed with him as he said: "Tom was wrong, perhaps. I hate the killing as badly as you do." A spark of his old fire seemed to flicker alive in him then, and, when he went on, his voice was sharper with that stubborn pride she knew so well. "Laura, no one can do this to Anchor and expect to get away with it. No one."

"Al Abbot did nothing to Anchor. Nor did Sam . . . or Ed." Her chin tilted stubbornly as she met his hard stare. "No one believes that. But it's true."

"Now, child, Tom Hale can prove they did it. He and Matt Briggs . . ."

"Tom Hale's word isn't worth the breath he wastes. He's a bully and he may be a liar."

John Worth was silent a moment. Finally he said: "I came in to ask you to come home with me, Laura. Now I can see that I was wrong in thinking you would."

"You were wrong in making me leave, Dad."

His back stiffened. "We'll argue that no further. I'm ashamed of what's come between us. People are beginning to talk." She could see him close his mind to her argument even before he said: "I won't be made a fool of, Laura. You wanted me to become one."

"Simply by letting a man you had mistreated take something you wanted?" She laughed, the harsh note of her voice lacking any merriment. "Dad, you made yourself smaller when you treated Sam as you did. Every day you keep on with it, you're only hurting yourself. If people are talking, it is to wonder how they could have respected John Worth all these years."

She had said enough. *Too much!* was her

frightening thought. She was suddenly afraid of having hurt him too deeply. Yet her pride wouldn't let her take back any of the things she had said, and, seeing how pointless it was to say anything further, she stepped on past him and into the cool lobby.

John Worth regarded the empty doorway thoughtfully, waiting there until his anger had quieted to the point where he was sure it wouldn't betray itself to anyone who saw him. Then he went down the steps and along the walk to the Congress, his back as ramrod straight as always.

Yesterday, on their way up to the line of the north fence, Al Abbot had pointed out the waste of the *malpais* to Ed. This twisted and writhing mass of cinder-black volcanic rock covered nearly a section of Sam Richards's land and continued on around the north shoulder of the mountains in a broadening belt that spread northwest across the butte-studded flats of the reservation. A thin top soil spotted the depressions, but for the most part the *malpais* was a bare solid mass of rock with steel-sharp edges so forbidding that animals seldom ventured into it because of the damage it did to their hoofs.

Ed had waited until the first light of the false dawn before heading into it, intending to hide his sign. He had cut four squares from the tarp of his bedroll and bound them about the brindle's

269

Schmaling Mem. Pub. Library
501 Tenth Avenue
Fulton, IL 61252

hoofs, tying them above the fetlock. He reasoned that news of the theft of Anchor's herd would certainly reach the reservation as soon as Sheriff Coombs could send it. If the agent co-operated with outside law, as he was supposed to, Len Avery's whereabouts would be of particular interest to him today. It followed that Avery, knowing he would be suspect, would be somewhere in plain sight, probably with an airtight alibi to give the agent when asked where he had spent night before last, the night Anchor's herd was driven off.

Riding the *malpais* was slow going and Ed went along carefully to save the gelding's hoofs. By mid-morning he had traveled only ten miles onto the reservation. When the black rock started giving out, he left it and rode openly. Once in the distance he saw a group of four riders angling along a trail ahead of him, but they showed no curiosity, and presently he watched the dust boil of their passage fade from sight against the heat-shimmering horizon. He crossed several well-defined trails but kept wide of them. Finally, with the sun directly overhead, he came to a rutted and well-traveled wagon road striking south around the east slope of the hills. He took it.

As he surmised, the road presently brought him within sight of a distant, sprawling cluster of wickiups and corrals roughly ringing several log buildings and one huge L-shaped structure of sun-baked adobe. He could only guess that this town was the heart of the reservation. A stream flowing down out of the juniper-studded foothills skirted the settlement and by the time he was fording it, an hour later, he had decided how he would go about this.

He rode boldly along the dusty, littered street, noticing that none of the Indians around the wickiups paid him the slightest attention. A faded sign over the door of the adobe building proclaimed that it was the agency and gave the name of the agent **T. S. HAVERS**. As he tied the brindle at the rail fronting the agency, one of the blue-uniformed reservation police lazed up off a bench alongside the broad doorway, leaving his carbine leaning against the wall.

"Havers in?" Ed asked but got nothing save a nod from the Indian who sat down once more, already losing interest in him.

Havers sat at a disorderly desk alongside the single window behind a railing dividing the front office. He was a dour-faced individual clad in a shiny suit of black serge and the glance he fixed on Ed as he entered was suspicious and reserved.

Ed decided to come straight to the point and bluff this through. He didn't give his name, didn't even say hello, instead asked brusquely: "Have you dug up anything for Coombs?"

The agent's face lost its guarded look immediately, and, as he rose from the desk and came to the rail, he said cordially: "Not a thing yet. But we have hopes."

Ed frowned, trying to appear disgusted. "A whole damn' herd walks across your layout here and all you can say is you have hopes."

"I'll give him anything I can," Havers was quick to say, his manner worried now, almost fawning. "But it's the same story it's been before. The cattle went straight on through. That country at the north end is just as wild as it was the first day the Maker created it. My police found tracks galore and the north fence cut. But nothing else, I'm afraid."

"So Anchor's beef got across into the next county?" Ed queried acidly.

The agent's bony shoulders lifted in a weary shrug. "I'm afraid so. I sent a man over there to get their sheriff busy on it."

"Were your police in on the deal?"

Havers appeared shocked and faintly angry. "Certainly not!"

"What about Avery? Where was he?"

"He's around. I talked to him this morning. But I can't check on his story. He had two men with him who swear he was at a sheep camp clear to hell and gone at the south end of the reservation the night the herd came through. They're both no-accounts and I wouldn't trust their word."

Hope was coming alive in Ed again. "How about my seeing him?"

"Avery?" The agent shrugged once more. "Why not? You'll probably find him loafing across at the store. He was there at noon when I went out to eat." As Ed turned toward the door, Havers added: "Sure wish there was something I could give you to go on. How's Bob Coombs? Who'd you say you were?"

Ed gave him a name, not his own. He permitted himself a spare smile as he led the brindle over to the log store obliquely across the dusty thoroughfare from the agency, mildly curious as to how a man as corrupt and inefficient as Havers managed his job. Havers had undoubtedly made only a faint pretense of checking Len Avery's story. Perhaps he was even in with Avery—or whoever was responsible for the theft of the herd.

The store's interior was as gloomy and dirty as Ed had expected, displaying cheap merchandise ranged along the counters and a clerk with a bald head and a sharp eye watching over it.

As Ed sauntered past him, the clerk said: "Something I can do for you?"

Ed didn't even bother answering. He was headed for a quartet of men sitting at a table under a window beyond one of the counters at the store's rear. They were playing a desultory game of cards, three Indians and a white man. The white man had the empty left sleeve of his grimy shirt doubled back and pinned at the shoulder.

Their incurious glances lifted from the cards to

273

watch Ed's approach. He caught Avery's eye and tilted his head toward the front of the barn-like room. "Have a word with you, Avery?"

The renegade laid the cards down carefully, then lifted his one hand and ran a finger along his wide mustache, his beady eyes watchful and running over Ed, yet avoiding any direct meeting of his glance.

Ed waited a long moment, then drawled: "Well, make up your mind."

"What's it about?" Avery asked finally, suspiciously.

"Hale sent me." He wondered what reaction his words would bring from the others, but, if they made any sense of what he was saying, they didn't show it.

Avery, however, opened his pale eyes a trifle wider and eased his caboose-chair back, rising, and telling the others: "Better deal me out."

He came on past Ed and led the way outside. He didn't stop until he had crossed the walk and could lean against the tie rail. Then he eyed Ed narrowly. "Tom ought to know better than to send a man straight in here for me."

"I came over to see Havers on business for the sheriff. He thinks I'm askin' you about night before last."

A smug smile played briefly over the renegade's ugly, hawk-like face. "That's better. What does Tom want?"

274

"Wants you to do another job like night before last. And like you did it on those horses," Ed drawled casually.

The suspicion flared in Avery's eyes once more. "Who might you be?"

"Hale and I used to travel together before he came here. He sent for me. Didn't want to trust any of the others this time."

Avery deliberately considered this for several seconds during which Ed schooled his expression to a steady impassiveness. Then, finally, Avery drawled: "OK. When does it come off?"

Here, then, was an admission of what Ed had suspected.

"Tonight," Ed said. "Help yourself to the first big batch you can round up."

Now Avery's glance probed Ed's directly for the first time. "Tonight? What the hell does Hale think I am, stickin' my neck out that far? They're on the prod across there."

"Tonight they'll be twenty miles south, combin' the trails below town," Ed lied blandly. "Hale's fixin' that."

"Why south? They know how we took the herd out."

"Hale's out after a man's scalp. Worth doesn't give much of a damn about the cattle he lost."

"Who's scalp? Sam Richards's?"

"No. A sidekick of Richards travelin' under the name of Nugent."

Avery smiled broadly. Then he seemed to think of something else, for his expression tightened once more with distrust. "How do I know Tom sent you?"

"Why would I be turnin' up with a story like this if he didn't?" Ed asked impatiently. "What's eatin' you? Ain't you getting enough out of this?"

The renegade was evidently satisfied. "I'm only bein' careful. Far as the money goes, nothin' could be better than keepin' it all like I did this last time, could it?"

Ed didn't answer, even though this was further proof of Avery's having done more than one job for Hale. He turned away and ducked under the rail, pulling loose his reins, and stepping up into the saddle. He looked down at Avery once more.

"Tom said to make it late. Right after midnight."

"OK," Avery said. "Only tell him this is the last batch Crawford can handle for a while. He's peddlin' those others to an outfit makin' up a trail herd that's headed into Wyoming."

"Tell Crawford to be careful," Ed drawled, the name meaning nothing to him. He reined on out into the street.

Going away, he resisted the impulse to look back at Avery. He let his breath out in a long, relieved sigh. He wondered if he could use what was happening tonight the way he had planned on using it.

IV

Sheriff Coombs had had a hard day—or rather a hard half a night and a day, for Tom Hale had routed him out of bed just before midnight last night. Now as he rode down to Lodgepole at dusk, he was as baffled and weary as he had ever been. His fourteen-man posse had accomplished exactly nothing during the day. Coombs felt like a fool. His common sense had argued all day that Sam had had nothing to do with the disappearance of Anchor's herd. Still, Hale had sworn out a warrant for the wrangler's arrest and it was a sheriff's duty to serve a warrant. So, after making Sam as comfortable as he could in the single cell, he brusquely told a few onlookers out front to clear the walk. Then he went up the street and gave Doc Simpson his keys and sent him back to the jail. Afterward he went to the hotel to eat and order Sam a meal.

Night had settled fully over Lodgepole when Coombs came back to the jail, carrying Sam's tray of food. The sheriff grumbled at sighting the jail's darkened window, wondering why Simpson hadn't had the sense to leave the desk lamp lit. He went on into his office, groped his way to the desk, set the tray down, and was reaching to a pocket for a match when a voice stopped him.

"Better pull the blinds first, Sheriff."

Coombs wheeled around so sharply that he nearly lost his balance. His hand stabbed half-way down to the .45 at his thigh before he caught himself and took it away again. He knew the voice and he knew that Ed Nugent wouldn't be fool enough to let himself be outdrawn or easily taken after having come here this way.

So Coombs did exactly as Ed had suggested, going to the window and drawing the blind there, then doing the same with the door's upper sash. As he moved back across the room, he began wondering where Nugent was standing. He struck his match and lit the lamp's wick and then turned to look behind him.

Ed sat tilted back in a chair in the room's front corner. His shell belt lay in his lap and his hands rested idly on the chair arms. His lean, tanned face was set seriously as he said: "Sheriff, I'm giving myself up. But on one condition."

Coombs was too surprised to speak at once. He swallowed with some difficulty before he managed to ask: "What is it?"

It took Ed all of five minutes to answer that, the lawman interjecting several questions and Sam Richards saying a thing or two from the cell. But at the end of that interval Ed came up out of the chair and walked to the desk, laying shell belt and gun on it.

The lawman watched this and, as Ed turned

from the desk, shook his head. "Better keep it, Nugent. You may need it."

"You're sure you want me to, Sheriff?"

"Dead sure."

John Worth caught the sound of several riders coming along the south trail and went outside to stand at the corner of the house. He recognized Laura when her horse cut through the pale wash of light spreading across the yard from the livingroom window. A warm feeling of relief and thankfulness ran through him. He was immediately curious when he saw that Bob Coombs followed Laura. The third rider, much taller than the lawman, Worth had never seen before. He stepped on out to the yard gate and called to Laura as she was swinging aground.

She came on to meet him, saying at once: "Are any of the men around, Dad?"

"No." He looked down at her, trying to make out her expression in the darkness. "Why?"

Instead of answering him, she turned and called to the other two who were hanging back in the deeper shadows: "It's all right."

"Something wrong, Laura?" the rancher asked, a worried premonition beginning to nag at him.

Before she could reply, Coombs and the tall man were walking up on them, the sheriff saying: "This is close enough. We don't want anyone surprising us."

"Why all the mystery, Bob?" Worth asked.

"John, meet Ed Nugent, the man that licked Hale," Coombs said without ceremony. "He's got something to tell you. You'd better let him get it said without trying to stop him."

Worth's ready temper came instantly on edge and stayed that way for perhaps a full minute as Ed began speaking. Then incredulity and amazement gradually thinned the rancher's anger. Several times he was on the point of interrupting but caught himself, remembering what Bob Coombs had said.

Ed finished by drawling: "So there you have it. Hale, for some reason, rigged it with Avery to steal those horses. Avery the same as admitted it outright this afternoon. You kicked Sam off the place and got his dander up. When he saw the chance of gettin' back at Hale, he bought that place out from under him. To get even with Sam for that, Hale framed him with this rustlin'."

"Another thing," Coombs said on the heel of Ed's words, "Avery mentioned a tie-up with a certain Crawford north of the reservation. You know any other Crawfords across there besides the sheriff, John?"

"No," Worth said quietly.

"Which is why nothin's ever been done about findin' the cattle that have strayed across there," the lawman said.

For several moments none of them spoke. Then

John Worth asked in a tight voice: "How can you prove all this, Nugent?"

"Take you up there to the break in the fence and have you watch Avery drive off your beef."

"You wouldn't be proving a thing that way," the rancher retorted. "Suppose you'd met Avery through Sam Richards instead of the way you say you did?"

"John, Nugent came in and offered to give himself up," Coombs growled. "If you're so bull-headed about it, we'll lock him up right here and go up there and corral Avery by ourselves. It's been a long time since I used my fists, but damned if I can't beat the truth out of that devil!"

"Dad," Laura said quietly. "Give in."

It was the pleading note of her voice, the half-pitying expression the faint light showed written on her face that suddenly brought home to John Worth the fact that he was being stubborn and a fool. He had his strong pride but it wilted now. His shoulders slumped and he lifted a hand and ran it across his face, saying wearily: "If it hadn't been for my telling Tom to push Sam Richards out, Al Abbot would still be alive."

Laura put a hand on his arm.

"Hell, yes," Coombs said gruffly. "But nothin's happened we can't mend, John. Hale was bound to kill somebody."

Watching the rancher, Ed saw his back stiffen. Then Worth was saying: "Laura, you stay here.

Tom planned on sleeping the crew at the Arrow Creek cabin tonight." He took out his watch and tilted its face so that the weak wash of lamplight from the living room caught it. "We have two hours before Avery takes those cattle through the fence. Plenty of time to get Hale and take him up there with us."

"How do you figure to do that, John?" Coombs asked.

"Don't know yet," Worth answered quietly. "But I'll manage it some way. I got to go in and get my Forty-Five."

They stood watching the rancher cross the yard and enter the house. As he disappeared, the lawman breathed fervently: "Here's hopin' we haven't stirred him up too much."

Ten minutes later the three of them rode out from Anchor's lower corral, the rancher insisting bluntly: "This is my affair from now on and I'm going at it my own way, Bob."

"Suit yourself."

"We're taking Tom up to the fence with us. Somehow we'll get our hands on Avery. When they're face to face, we can make them talk. One's sure to sell out the other."

"It might work at that," the sheriff said.

They climbed the ridge trail and Worth rode point for Arrow Creek. And when, forty minutes later, they looked down through the trees and made out the light of the line shack's window,

Worth said softly: "There's no point in tipping our hand to Tom. I'll go on down alone and tell him he's needed back at the house. You two can wait along the trail below and jump us as we come out."

Without pausing for them to answer, he lifted rein and headed down through the pines. He was gone for nearly a quarter hour. Finally they heard the sound of a horse coming in on them, and Coombs drew his Colt and stepped down out of the saddle. But as it turned out his precaution was unnecessary. For John Worth was riding the trail alone.

"Tom and Briggs pulled out about an hour ago," he told them worriedly. "They were headed back to the layout, according to the others. Sandy said Tom had something to talk over with me. I'd better get back there."

"One man's enough to make sure Avery takes those cattle through the fence," Ed put in. "Why not let him go? You can always gather him in later. Let Avery run those cattle across there, and, when we trail him, you'll have the proof you want on Crawford."

Coombs nodded, asking: "How does that sound, John?"

"Like sense," Worth replied, lifting rein. "Let's get on back to Anchor."

When they headed on down the trail, Worth was in the lead, setting a fast pace.

• • •

Back along Arrow Creek trail, Matt Briggs's horse had gone lame and he and Tom Hale had stopped while he pried a stone from his bay's left fore-hoof. It was just as Briggs was climbing back into his saddle that they caught the echo of horses. They had pulled off into the pines and watched three riders go by at a stiff trot. Hale recognized only one—John Worth.

As far as Tom Hale knew, Worth had been alone at the ranch most of the day. Even the cook had joined the posse for the hunt. So the Anchor foreman had been at once curious and wary over who the pair siding Worth might be.

"We'll go on in," he had told Briggs uncertainly, hardly knowing what this could mean. They had ridden on to Anchor to find the house lighted and Laura alone there. The oddity of finding John Worth's daughter back home again added to Tom Hale's feeling of disquiet. For a while, after finding Laura there in the living room, he restlessly paced the yard by the bunkhouse, trying to reason out an explanation for the half-frightened way the girl had spoken to him. She had never particularly liked him, he knew, but her manner had been different just now, her aloofness replaced by something he was almost sure was fear. She had come out to see her father, she said, and had found the house deserted.

Finally Hale decided she hadn't told him the

284

truth. He called to Briggs: "Matt, pick yourself a spot out here and watch things. Something's goin' on we don't know about."

In the living room the girl had thrown two fresh rounds of pine on the fire and it was blazing now, sending a flickering light out across the room, thinning the shadows the lamplight from the center table didn't reach.

As Hale closed the door, he noticed the wary way her glance touched him and dropped away as she said: "Yes, Tom?"

"I'm worried about your father," he said. "Where could he have gone?"

"Any number of places," was her cool reply. "He might even have taken the lower trail to town and missed meeting me."

"Why would he want to go to town?"

A humorless smile drew out the fine line of her lips. "Why would that be your business?" she asked.

He ignored that. "Something could have happened to him."

"Could it?"

Her sureness told him something—she had seen her father, and, thinking back, trying his best to remember the look of the riders who had been with John Worth, his impatience to know what lay behind Laura's strange manner all at once got the best of him.

"You've seen him tonight, haven't you?" he queried abruptly.

Fear momentarily touched her glance, giving way to an indignant look. "Aren't you forgetting yourself, Tom? I said I hadn't seen him."

Suddenly a thought struck Hale and he was breathing—"Nugent."—knowing now who that tall rider with Worth had been.

Laura's face paled as she asked: "What was that you said?"

"Nugent and the sheriff, maybe," he said in a brittle tone. And the quick alarm that came to her blue eyes told him that his guess was close to the mark.

He started toward her and she came up out of the chair, a look of wild fright crossing her face. "What are you doing?" she asked quickly, then stepped in behind the chair and started backing toward the door to the house's bedroom wing, her eyes wide and a sudden look of loathing in them.

He lunged for her then, and caught her as she was going through the door, swinging her roughly against the wall. He struck her sharply, hard across the face with an open palm.

"You little hellcat," he rasped. "Where were they headed? Talk, or I'll . . ."

A sound behind him suddenly brought him wheeling around, his big fist dropping from Laura's arm and streaking toward holster, then freezing within finger spread of his Colt.

Ed Nugent's tall shape filled the doorway. He

stood, spraddle-legged, a cold smile on his angular, lean face.

"Go ahead, Hale. Make your try." Ed's drawl was soft, almost gentle.

Tom Hale held, motionless as rock. An instant ago he had remembered the blurred speed with which this stranger had drawn on Sandy there on the hotel porch, and he knew with a terrible certainty that he was dead the moment his hand touched his .45.

"Go ahead," Ed drawled once more tauntingly.

Hale squared away at him, being careful with his hands. "Why should I?" he asked tonelessly.

Now, from Hale's left, came the faint squeak of metal grating against metal and the Anchor foreman's glance shuttled quickly to that side of the room to see the kitchen door swing open.

Bob Coombs came through the door, halting just clear of it. His hand fisted a .45 that was leveled at Hale. He said sharply: "Come across here, Laura."

The girl's face was chalk-white as she edged out from the wall, stepped around Hale's back, and started across the room.

Ed said: "Unbuckle your belt, Hale. Then we'll see how easy you come apart."

A naked, sickening fear showed on Tom Hale's bruised face now. "What's this you're tryin' to do to me?" he asked helplessly, summoning what anger he could and trying to look indignant. "I was only . . ."

All at once a gun exploded hollowly across the night outside. A hard blow struck Ed in the back, spinning him halfway around. He lurched on into the room and at that instant Hale, seeing that Laura stood between him and the sheriff, whipped a hand to his holstered Colt.

Ed threw himself into a sideward roll. His left shoulder—where Matt Briggs's bullet had slammed into him—hit the floor and a blinding pain flooded through his upper body the instant Tom Hale's gun blasted apart the room's silence. The air impact of the bullet stirred Ed's shirt along his back. Then he was firing his gun.

A blow at his chest slammed him back against the wall. Coombs was stepping from behind Laura, trying to get in a shot as Ed fired a second time. Hale's mouth sagged open, an expression of bewilderment and rage crossing his face. But his eyes were already taking on a blank look as he buckled at the waist and toppled off balance, going head down onto the floor.

Laura's horror-stricken glance swept on across to Ed. She cried out softly and ran across to him, kneeling beside him as Coombs went to look at Hale. A quick boot tread sounded crossing the porch outside and a moment later John Worth hurried into the room.

"Dad, help me," Laura said, choking back a sob. She was looking helplessly down at Ed, whose head lay against the boards. Nugent's fingers had lost their grip on the .45 and his long frame had a look of looseness quite like that of Tom Hale's and there was a bright splotch of crimson patterning his shirt at the left shoulder.

John Worth said gravely—"Here, I'll do it."— and knelt beside her to roll Ed gently over onto his back.

Coombs came across the room and stood looking down at them, bleakly drawling: "Hale's so much coyote bait." He saw Worth open the lid of Ed's left eye. "Fainted, hasn't he, John?"

The rancher nodded. "Laura, go get some hot water and a clean cloth." He looked up at her, a slow smile patterning his thin face. "And don't worry. He's going to be kickin' around a long while yet."

She let her breath out in a sob of thankfulness and her father gave her a startled look as he was unbuttoning Ed's shirt and drawing it away from the wounded shoulder. "What's come over you, child?"

The way her face reddened, the hurried way she rose and went to the kitchen, made Worth glance up at the sheriff soberly.

"Damned if you can blame her, John," the lawman said positively. "You should've seen him. Fast. And both shots dead center. . . ." He sobered then, eyeing Worth oddly, respectfully. "Was that Briggs you ran into outside?"

John Worth nodded, nothing more. Then he took a closer look at Ed's shoulder, sighing in relief. "It's a clean hole. No bones broken."

He looked around then as Laura came back into the room carrying a basin of water and a clean towel. She was kneeling beside him again when he asked: "Do you suppose Nugent would want to work here?"

"He's got work, Dad," Laura told him. "With Sam Richards."

"Sam can get another man," John Worth said gruffly. He gave his daughter a sideward, mock-serious glance. "Now I'm not counting on you, Laura. You can help Sam out, like you've done a job helping me on Anchor an' lately even with myself . . . but I still need a man on this spread. Will you let your father do something right for a change . . . ?"

Additional copyright information:

"A Tinhorn Takes a Tank Town" first appeared in *Western Story* Magazine (4/9/38). Copyright © 1938 by Street & Smith Publications, Inc. Copyright © renewed 1966 by Dorothy S. Ewing. Copyright © 2005 by Dorothy S. Ewing for restored material.

"Unwanted Gold" first appeared under the title "Gun Destiny of the Branded" in *Western Novel and Short Stories* (5/39). Copyright © 1939 by Newsstand Publications, Inc. Copyright © renewed 1967 by Dorothy S. Ewing. Copyright © 2005 by Dorothy S. Ewing for restored material.

"Hell for Homesteaders" first appeared in *Western Story Magazine* (11/5/38). Copyright © 1938 by Street & Smith Publications, Inc. Copyright © renewed 1966 by Dorothy S. Ewing. Copyright © 2005 by Dorothy S. Ewing for restored material.

"Back-Trail Betrayal" first appeared in *Western Story Magazine* (3/26/38). Copyright © 1938 by Street & Smith Publications, Inc. Copyright © renewed 1966 by Dorothy S. Ewing. Copyright © 2005 by Dorothy S. Ewing for restored material.

"Showdown at Anchor" first appeared under the title "A Man for Hell's Canyon" in *Fifteen Western Tales* (11/47). Copyright © 1947 by Popular Publications, Inc. Copyright © renewed 1975 by Dorothy S. Ewing. Copyright © 2005 by Dorothy S. Ewing for restored material.

About the Author

Peter Dawson is the *nom de plume* used by Jonathan Hurff Glidden. He was born in Kewanee, Illinois, and was graduated from the University of Illinois with a degree in English literature. In his career as a Western writer he published sixteen Western novels and wrote over 120 Western short novels and short stories for the magazine market. From the beginning he was a dedicated craftsman who revised and polished his fiction until it shone as a fine gem. His Peter Dawson novels are noted for their adept plotting, interesting and well-developed characters, their authentically researched historical backgrounds, and his stylistic flair. During the Second World War, Glidden served with the U.S. Strategic and Tactical Air Force in the United Kingdom. Later in 1950 he served for a time as Assistant to Chief of Station in Germany. After the war, his novels were frequently serialized in *The Saturday Evening Post*. Peter Dawson titles such as *Gunsmoke Graze*, *Royal Gorge*, and *Ruler of the Range* are generally conceded to be among his best titles, although he was an extremely consistent writer, and virtually all his fiction has retained its classic stature among readers of all generations. One of Jon Glidden's finest techniques was his ability, after the fashion of Dickens and Tolstoy, to tell his stories via a series of dramatic vignettes which focus on a wide assortment of different characters, all tending to develop their own lives, situations, and predicaments, while at the same time propelling the general plot of the story toward a suspenseful conclusion. He was no less gifted as a master of the short novel and short story. *Dark Riders of Doom* (Five Star Westerns, 1996) was the first collection of his Western short novels and stories to be published.

Center Point Large Print
600 Brooks Road / PO Box 1
Thorndike, ME 04986-0001 USA

(207) 568-3717

US & Canada:
1 800 929-9108
www.centerpointlargeprint.com

Schmaling Mem. Pub. Library
501 Tenth Avenue
Fulton, IL 61252